Magic & Menopause

THE ORACLE OF WYNTER

USA TODAY BESTSELLING AUTHOR

LISA MANIFOLD

MAGIC & MENOPAUSE

THE ORACLE OF WYNTER BOOK TWO

LISA MANIFOLD

CHAPTER ONE

$\mathcal{I}$ stared at the doctor, the disorientation hitting hard. "You want to do what?" Usually she made my yearly physical seem like visiting with a friend, but this time, not.

I didn't know what was wrong with me this afternoon, but I'd been asking people to repeat themselves far too often. My daughter, my best friend Shelly, even the the receptionist when she'd asked for my payment earlier, and now my doctor, Dr. Chloe Amberson. Everyone seemed to speak a shorthand I could not comprehend.

"Wynter, we can find out if this is menopause pretty easily." She gave me her you-know-you've-got-to-do-this smile. "We'll take some blood, and that's all.

Voila!" She nodded like I'd already agreed. "Then we'll know, one way or another." Her voice is bouncy and bright to disguise the grenade she's setting off in my life.

"It can't be menopause." My forehead crinkled. "It just... can't." I had powers, magic supposedly. Not menopause. Magic. Couldn't I stop this? Wasn't there some kind of anti-aging potion?

"Why? Because the hot flashes are symptomatic of say, gout?" Dr. Amberson's words hit me all wrong, wrong, wrong. "Are you cold?"

"I'm sorry, what?" Her sudden change of subject threw me off.

"Right now. Are you cold?"

"No, which is weird. Normally, I'm freezing in here." I indicated the sweater sitting on the chair opposite me under my purse. Then I looked up at Dr. Amberson. My mouth was partially open, probably shock.

"You're just proving my point."

"I cannot be in menopause." I stared off at the wall. This would be one more damn thing in this month of damn things.

"You're ahead of the game if you find out when all you're dealing with is hot flashes."

"What else is there?" I asked. Like the hot flashes weren't bad enough? There was more? "I'm too young for this. I'm not even fifty."

"We all go through it." She patted my shoulder. "I survived. You'll survive."

The fluorescent light in the room crackled, which made me jump. All of a sudden, I could smell the alcohol in the sanitizer she'd used when she'd first come in, sharp and biting. I could smell the air conditioning in the room, even if I didn't feel it. But I knew I wasn't pregnant, which was the last time I noticed things crazy like this.

Oh, God. Menopause.

"Let's take some blood, and then we'll know." She was all business.

"What else can I expect?"

"Hmm?" Dr. Amberson held up the needle she had in her hand.

"What else can I expect from menopause?" I repeated myself, wanting to make sure I'd get the information I needed. "Other symptoms, that kind of thing."

"Oh," she turned around, needle still in hand. "You tend to sweat more at night. Weight gain, and your metabolism shifts. Insomnia. Don't worry about it right now, Wynter." Her smile dropped away. "Wait. You haven't been looking up your symptoms, have you?" Her eyes got fierce.

Whoa.

"No. I haven't looked up a thing." I wasn't lying. Like I'd admit it if I was. She was downright scary at the moment.

With everything that had been going on—the death of my husband in a helicopter crash, learning he had another life, another wife, and even other kids, for one thing. Then helping my own kids deal with these facts about their father. That was still tough.

Add to that finding out that I was a magical being called the Oracle of Theama, with Logan (a consultant seeking my help as the Oracle) and Florry (the former Oracle)—my recent hot flashes had just been one more annoying thing I needed to deal with. I didn't have the time to look into them. My sweating just wasn't high on my list of concerns.

With what I'd been through the last month, I felt like sweating more than normal was appropriate. I'd already escaped being killed by random scary men.

"Good. When you start to search via search engines or medical websites for reasons for your symptoms, you either have cancer, or you're going to die soon," Dr. Amberson said, bringing me back to our conversation.

Despite my stress over the idea that I might be in menopause, I laughed. "I used to see that when I'd look up things for the kids."

She rolled her eyes. "The people who write most of the medical symptoms should lose internet privileges. I get more people in here scared to death based on something they read."

"So you're saying I should be grateful it's just menopause?"

"Not at all. Menopause is just another step in the female reproductive system, one that requires us to manage it and live with it. It's not fun."

"Par for the course," I said.

"Exactly. So my job is to find out if that is what this really is and help you ease the symptoms. I don't believe in just having to live with it."

Hearing her, with her matter-of-fact approach, made me feel better.

"Which arm?" Dr. Amberson waved the needle at me.

I stuck out my right arm, pushing up my sleeve.

There was a silence.

"When did you get a tattoo?" Dr. Amberson asked.

"What?" I looked down. How in the hell had I forgotten it was there? "Oh, a while ago," I said.

What could I say? That I was in the middle of an act of angry midlife crisis, which landed me in the hotel room of a guy I'd just met, and he'd disappeared, and I'd found this bracelet shoved in the cushion of a chair and when I'd put it on, I blacked out and woke up with a tattoo? Yeah, no. Not in a million years.

Even though that was exactly what had happened.

And the tattoo, Goldie (named by one of the former Oracles), was not just any old tattoo. He—I called it a he, even though Goldie himself hadn't actually told me if he was a he or a she—talked, and was part of a magical responsibility that landed on me when I put the bracelet on. I was, as I mentioned, the Oracle of Theama, a descendent of the Oracle of Delphi, the person the supernatural world turned to when they needed answers.

Well, after they'd proven themselves worthy of my time. At least that was what Logan, my first consultant, told me. He could have been lying, but Florry, who was a… what was Florry? She was the previous Oracle, and she hovered around as a ghost who showed up at what seemed to be less than optimal times. But she said that we—the Oracles—were protected. Sort of. I still wasn't clear on how the protection of the Oracle worked.

No, I couldn't tell Dr. Amberson any of this. Better for her to believe that I'd gotten a wild hair and run off to a tattoo shop.

"It's beautiful," Dr. Amberson said. "The detail is superb."

"Thank you," I said. I could feel Goldie stirring along my arm. There was no communication from him, although I could sense his pleasure. He listened in far more than I would like. It gave new meaning to the words 'never alone'.

"Okay, just a pinch," Dr. Amberson said. She stuck the needle in, and I jumped. "Can you wait? The lab isn't all that busy right now, so I can find out the answer today." She smiled.

"What? Oh, yes, I can wait," I said.

"Okay, I'll have you wait out in the front office," Dr. Amberson said. "This won't take long. I'll call you back as soon as I have the results."

I nodded, following her out of the exam room, and let my mind drift. This week had been full of chores after we'd come back from Phoenix, and I'd been falling into bed with my eyes closed before I hit the pillow the last several nights. Which was good. Ever since finding Goldie the armband and taking on the responsibility of being the Oracle, the Oracle of Theama, to be specific, I'd had a lot of dreams that were related to the quest of my first consultant, Logan Gentry.

A dreamless night was a gift now.

Unbidden, my mind went to last week, when the kids and I'd had finally made the trip to Phoenix. We'd gone there to see Natalie Chastain, who had also been married to my late husband, Derek. He had two wives, and neither of us knew about the other one. Which sounds crazy, but he worked as a tour guide in the Grand Canyon six months a year, and he had, I'd discovered, kept a separate set of books in order to support Natalie and her kids. As small as that fact was, it made me feel a little better. I'd kept the books for years. I couldn't figure out how I'd missed a second family.

Back to Natalie Chastain and her kids. Yes, she had kids. Two very cute kids, Nathan and Sophie. Which is why I was in Phoenix with my kids, Theo, Kris, and Rachel. They wanted to meet their younger siblings. I'd gotten the impression that Natalie Chastain was about as thrilled as I was at the idea of this meeting. Also known as not enthusiastic at all.

The things you do for your kids.

We'd pulled into the driveway, and the two younger children were at the door. I could see a tall woman behind them, hidden in the shadow of the house. Everyone got out of the car and walked slowly up the front sidewalk.

The boy spoke first. "I'm Nathan Chastain. You have the same dad we do."

There was silence from my three, and then Theo spoke. "Yes, we do. I'm really sorry that he's not here anymore."

Neither of the younger children replied immediately. Then the girl, Sophie, said, "Even though he lied to all of us?"

"Did you love him any less?" Rachel asked. Her tone was gentle, which surprised me. She'd been the angriest of my three at her father.

Sophie slowly shook her head, and I could see the shimmer of tears in her eyes. One snuck down her face, dripping off her cheek. Sophie didn't seem to notice. "I'm mad at him, though. Mommy cried." Her voice was soft, barely above a whisper.

Nathan slid his hand into his sister's. I saw the motion, as did my kids, and something about the mood softened. I couldn't tell what it was, exactly, but my kids knew that support, knew what was going on.

"Why don't we invite our guests in?" a soft voice from behind the kids said.

Natalie Chastain stepped into the light.

She was as pretty as my social media snooping told me she was. And tall—she had to be five-nine or five-ten, at least. I felt short and old. Because Natalie was younger than I was. By at least ten years. Maybe more, but I wasn't going to give her that.

It would mean she met Derek in her twenties.

I sighed and resisted the urge to fan myself. Phoenix was *hot.*

"I'm Wynter," I said, sticking out my hand. "And these are my children, Theo, Rachel, and Kris." I nodded at my kids. "We're very glad to meet you."

"Are you?" Nathan asked, his face serious as he shook my hand. I didn't see any ill will, only genuine curiosity.

"Okay, we really need to take this off the front porch," Natalie said, her eyes sliding left and right. There were no neighbors in sight, but clearly, she was self-conscious. "Please come in." She moved back into the shadow of the house, and the kids stepped away from the door.

We walked in and the door closed behind us.

"Please come in," Natalie said again. "I have coffee, and tea in the kitchen." Even in the darker room, I could see the flush of her cheeks. She wasn't comfortable with this.

Well, who would be? Meeting your late husband's first wife? What was the etiquette for that? Not in Emily Post, not that I could remember.

No one spoke as we walked into the kitchen. Natalie's home had a warm, comfortable southwestern style that was miles different from my New England seaside cottage look. I liked it, though. It fit her.

I wanted to hate this woman. Really, truly. I wanted to hate her and write her off and never think of her again. Then I saw the expressions on my kids' faces and remembered why I'd made a different call.

"Please have a seat," Natalie said, her hand waving to a large table with a long bench on one side, and chairs on the other three sides. Nathan and Sophie went immediately to the bench.

Kris sat down next to them, smiling as he did so.

Natalie sat at the head of the table, next to her children. I took the seat next to her. Rachel was by my side, and Theo sat down on Rachel's other side.

I felt Rachel's hand give mine a squeeze under the table. I hid a smile. "Thank you for inviting us," I said. Since the little kids had tossed the ball out, I could be as brave. "I know this couldn't have been easy. It wasn't easy for us." My eyes slid past Natalie's and to her children. "But we believe in brothers and sisters. So we had to come and see you. Which is why I am glad to meet you."

"Thank you," Natalie said quietly.

I didn't know whether to be glad for or curse her stillness.

"So what now?" Sophie asked.

"How about some tea? And can I have a cookie? Maybe two?" Kris asked.

"Sure," Sophie nodded. "We made them this morning."

"We didn't poison them or anything," Nathan added.

His mother shot him a 'you're so dead later' glare.

"In case you were wondering," Nathan added, squirming in his seat.

There was a moment of silence, and then Theo burst into laughter. Kris joined him, and even Rachel, who had maintained a cool civility up to this point, smiled.

"Well, that's good to know," I said. "Being poisoned wasn't on our to-do list today."

Sophie giggled, and Nathan smiled, although he was still watching his mom.

But Natalie was smiling. It wasn't a big smile, but it was a smile.

I felt myself relax a little as my shoulders dropped away from my ears. When people smile when they don't really want to, you can't help but be hopeful. I knew, right then, that I would never be able to hate her, not unless she told me she knew Derek was married.

Even then, I knew the hate would fade. Even now, while things were still fresh, it felt like a lot of effort to carry hate around. She wasn't a bad person. These kids weren't bad kids.

Derek had done wrong to us all.

I reached over and put my hand on Natalie's. "I know that it may seem strange, but I just can't be mad at you. As much as I want to be," I added ruefully.

Her smile broadened, one side of her mouth tilting up crookedly. "I would like to hate you, too, for the record." She sighed heavily, looking down at her hands. "But I'm not made that way, and I don't think you're any more to blame for this than I am."

None of the kids spoke. All five of them were listening to us.

"No, you're not," Rachel said. "This was all Dad."

Sophie's eyes went round, and Nathan's face sobered immediately. Kris and Theo watched their sister carefully.

"But that doesn't mean we have to keep screwing this up like he did," Rachel said. "We can be honest with each other and make things better. No more secrets," she looked around the table.

"You think he screwed things up?" Nathan asked.

"Rachel," I said.

"Yes, I do. Do you think this is how people should do things? Because I don't," Rachel said. "But we don't have to make the same mistakes." She ignored me.

"No more secrets," Sophie said, nodding her head.

"So what did you say when you found out about us?" Nathan asked.

"A lot of cuss words," Rachel said with no hesitation. "Most of them directed at Dad."

"Mommy yelled," Nathan said. "Then cried."

"I think Mom cried too," Theo said. "We don't live with her anymore, so I think she stopped crying before we came to see her."

"Where do you live?" Nathan asked.

"Why don't you live with your mommy?" Sophie asked at the same time.

"Mom still lives on the Vineyard. We all moved off island after college," Kris said. "Easier for jobs."

Natalie nodded. "That makes sense. Please, have some cookies. Otherwise, we'll eat them all and then no one will sleep tonight."

The eternal worry of the mother.

The mood was lighter as everyone ate the non-poisoned cookies. After a while, the younger kids got restless, and my three went with them out back to see the pool and play area.

Leaving me and Natalie alone.

Something I didn't think either of us was jazzed about.

"Thank you—" I began.

"Thank you," she said at the same time.

We both stopped and laughed a little.

"Go ahead," I said.

"Thank you for coming out. For being gracious. My kids were really worried that you'd be angry at us, because you were here first."

"I was," I said. "This turned my life upside down in a way I didn't expect."

She nodded. "I understand that. Maybe you and I will never be at ease, but I want something more for my kids. I don't have any brothers or sisters. I was an only child, and my parents both died while I was in college. They were so excited at the idea of having family, even as they were nervous about what you thought. Derek never talked about his family. I always thought they were estranged."

Damn this woman. I could see why Derek liked her. I liked her, and I didn't want to. She was a nice woman.

Damn it.

"No, they're still alive," I said. "And they will be delighted to know about more grandkids. Derek has two sisters, but neither of them ever had children."

"How do you feel about that?" Natalie asked.

"Part of me hurts for my kids. Will it change the way their grandparents see them? My parents are gone, too, so Derek's parents are all they have left," I said. I felt kind of small, but I wanted to be honest. "But your kids deserve to know their grandparents, and Maud and Donovan are both wonderful people," I added.

"I can't believe he never told me about them," she said, a slight frown making the middle of her forehead crinkle.

"I'm sorry," I said. I mean, what else could I say?

She sighed. "How can I miss him so much when I'd beat him to death if I saw him again?"

I shrugged, laughing. "I don't know. All I can say is I know how you feel." I stopped, not sure how much to say. "I pulled all his clothes out of the closet, dumped them on the floor, and had the kids cart them away."

A puff of laughter burst out from Natalie, almost unwillingly. "Thank you," she said,

And for the first time since I'd come in, our eyes met in perfect understanding.

This might not be easy, and it would probably be bumpy as we found our way into this new reality, but it would be all right. Eventually.

I smiled now, in the doctor's office, thinking about that weekend, ignoring the flush of heat that was rising up from my feet. The visit had been far less awkward than anyone expected it to be. Rachel emailed both of the kids every day. Natalie had been right—the younger kids were delighted to have siblings.

I'd taken a day and gone to see Maud and Donovan, who lived in New York, after I'd come home from Phoenix, and told them the news. They'd been shocked, and angry, and then, just as we were, curious about Derek's other wife, and then anxious to meet their newest grandchildren. When I'd talked with Maud last week, there were plans being made for visits. I'd left it to my in-laws to tell Derek's sisters.

I was glad for Nathan and Sophie that their newfound grandparents were all in. I knew that Maud and Donovan were deeply hurt by Derek's actions, but that wasn't something I could manage.

I had enough on my plate, thank you very much.

If you are past your time of breeding, your magic will be enhanced, I heard a thin, high voice say.

"Great. Thanks, Goldie. That totally makes up for all the other benefits of menopause." I spoke out loud without thinking, only remembering I was out in public after I spoke. Damn it. I snuck a glance around the waiting room. Only one young woman looked up at me, and I smiled, looking back down at my phone in my hand. She returned the smile and her eyes went back to her own phone.

That was close. Good grief. I needed to keep a better guard on myself.

What other benefits? he asked.

Clearly, Goldie didn't always catch the sarcasm.

I was saved from an answer by Dr. Amberson poking her head out of the hallway that led to the exam rooms. "Come on back," she said.

Getting up, I glanced around the waiting room. It wasn't busy today, but a woman came in as I walked by the front door. Her hair was the rich, creamy blonde that screamed money and monthly hair appointments. She turned to face the waiting room, and I stumbled.

It was Davina from the party. Davina in the golden dress, who had clung to Evander—Logan—as though he were an accessory. Her gaze slid past me with no recognition even as she looked carefully at me. And why would she? It was my dream.

But what was this woman, this sort of woman, doing here, on Martha's Vineyard? Seeing a doctor, as though she lived here? A ripple of fear moved through me, threatening to engulf me. I'd have to tell Logan. If she saw him, she'd blow his hiding place. I didn't know if he wanted to resume his life as Evander Thane, but he should be the one to make that choice, not this woman or anyone else.

Sweet baby Jee. I couldn't even go to my lady bits doctor without my Oracle world pushing in. Was this how it was going to be from now on? Being the Oracle would take over everything?

I wasn't sure I liked that.

Lost in thoughts of my future and worry over what Davina was doing here, I didn't pay attention as we walked down the hallway. I walked in through the open doorway, unseeing, as Dr. Amberson stopped at a door to one of the exam rooms. I sat down, still seeing the blond hair and aloof expression of Davina.

"I have the results," Dr. Amberson said, looking down at the chart in her hand and then up at me, a slight smile on her face. "It's official. You're in menopause."

Wonderful.

hen I got home from the doctor's, it was with a bag of Chinese food tucked under my arm. The news of my impending menopause, the cryptic warning from Goldie about magic, and the sighting of Davina had made me crave nothing but comfort food. This time, there was no darkly handsome man lounging on my porch to scare the daylights out of me and make me drop my food, so I was able to curl up on the couch and eat every one of the Hunan scallops all by myself.

They were delicious. I fell asleep watching the news, and I woke up because the crick in my neck was screaming. And I was sweating. A lot.

"God," I groaned. I tidied up, downed a glass of water, and then refilled it and took it up with me, just in case. You know, because menopause. Dr. Amberson had told me more than once to drink more water.

My eyes were closed as I pulled the blankets up to my chin. I could feel myself settle down into the mattress, the harbinger of sleep for me.

A loud screech and a thump had me sitting straight up in bed, the hair on my arms and the back of my neck all at attention.

"What the hell? Goldie?" I asked, hoping for some insight.

This isn't good, Goldie said.

"You think?" I hissed. "What is it?"

Hide!

I got out of bed and was heading for one of the closets when the door slammed opened. The heat I'd felt before bed was replaced with a cold sweat. I felt something hard hit me in the back between the shoulders, almost scooping me as I was hit. I flew backward and fell, half on, half off the bed.

"Give it to me," a feminine voice said. The lightness of the voice was belied by the anger and determination I heard in the few words.

"Who are you? Get out of my house," I wheezed, finding it hard to catch my breath, much less get up and see who had just attacked me.

I heard a clopping, like hobnailed boots, coming closer. A large shadow loomed over me, and a rank smell of the barnyard filled the room.

"Oh, for Pete's sake!" I tried to yell. I knew who it was then. The bull and the damn woman—what was her name? Adriane? No, Ariadne. "You're not getting the armband! I'm the Oracle! I accepted it! It's mine, and you can't have it! Now get out of my house!" I managed to push myself up with my hands behind me against the bed, and unlike the last time she was here, I wasn't frightened.

I was furious.

"This should have never come to you," Ariadne said, her voice still musical. "A less likely candidate for the Oracle has never been chosen." She shook her head.

The bull, on two legs, edged closer to Ariadne. Her hand reached up to stroke the bull's front paw—arm? —absently. He snorted.

"Gack," I said. "You need a good dentist. As for you," I looked at Ariadne, "I don't know that you're one to make judgements about the Oracle."

Ariadne glared. "Don't insult him. It makes him angry." She smiled, her dark curls falling around her face. The musical sound of her voice took on an evil note. "Or have you forgotten the last time he paid you a visit?"

"I haven't forgotten a thing!" I flared. "Nor have I forgotten how you both ran from here, tails between your legs, when you met my friend."

"Where is the panther tonight?" Ariadne jeered.

Logan was in New York, tracking down his under the radar colleagues to help him hack his Swiss bank accounts. At least, that's what he'd told me. Since I'd technically solved his question—to find his past—and revealed that he was a man named Evander Thane, our quest together was at an end. He owed me nothing. But he said he was coming back, and quest or no quest, I was glad. His things were still in the small guest bedroom, indicating that he hadn't taken off. I didn't know what it meant. But I was still glad.

"I don't need him," I said, standing up tall. "I can take care of you on my own. Because I am the Oracle, and we do not take kindly to threats from the likes of you." If I hadn't been so mad at the audacity of this chick, I would have laughed at myself.

"Rixte ton istó pàno tis," Ariadne said in a tone barely above a whisper.

Close your eyes, Goldie shouted. *Close them now, Wynter!*

I closed my eyes, but I could still hear Ariadne chanting.

"Rixte ton istó pàno tis, rixte ton istó pàno tis, rixte ton istó pàno tis!" Her voice rose to a shout on the last recitation.

What felt like mist settled upon me. I forced myself to hold still, even though all I wanted to do was rub at my arms and hair at whatever magic she was hexing me with. I didn't know how I knew, but this was a hex.

The bull stamped and snorted. I could feel the heat of his warm, stinky breath. Eww. I was never going to get the smell out.

Out.

Wait. I could get them out of here. I opened my eyes and glared, thinking about sending Ariadne and the bull far, far away.

But as I glared, they both disappeared, leaving me feeling like I was coated in a covering of glue, and a haze of bad breath.

"What in the hell?" I asked.

Get to your shower. See if it washes off, Goldie commanded.

"Why are you never this forceful when it could help me?" I asked. "Like with some super-secret spell, or something?"

He made a noise that sounded like disgust, but didn't reply.

I opened my windows, even though it was chilly tonight, and then went into the bathroom to take the hottest shower known to man. By the time the water ran cold, I didn't feel like there was a coating of something on my skin, but whatever she'd tossed at me, it was still there. Not as present as when she'd chanted and mist settled all around me, but still very much there. Great.

"I'm not going to grow warts, or die in some hideously embarrassing fashion, am I?" I asked as I was drying off, hoping Goldie was over his snit.

I don't know, he said. *It would be nice if Florry would put in an appearance. This is more her area of knowledge than my own.*

"Yes, it would. Florry!" I yelled as I toweled off my hair.

There was no response. I grumbled to myself as I put on fresh pajamas and got back into bed. "How am I supposed to sleep after this?" I asked out loud.

Goldie didn't answer, for which I was glad.

I didn't really want an answer. I closed my eyes, hoping I'd at least be able to rest.

When I opened my eyes again, it was morning. The sun shone in my window, and the curtains billowed with the breeze. The blankets on the bed were slightly damp, but that was a price I was willing to pay to not have Stinky the Bull's breath lingering in my room.

What was it with stinky people coming after me? First the guy Logan had called Stinky, the one he said was a necromancer, that I'd sent who-knows-where when he'd broken into my house and tried to take Goldie. Now this damn bull.

Maybe the people with bad intentions stank? It was something to keep in mind. I'd pay closer attention moving forward.

I pulled the grimoire from where I kept it at night, under the blankets and next to me in bed. "Okay, it's time for hard talk, ladies. What is with that lady and her bull? Why is she still bothering me? I know you all tend to be light on the answers, but I need something."

I turned the pages slowly, willing someone—any of the previous Oracles—to give me something. "I really need help today," I said, enunciating clearly. "Because this isn't going to work if I have to air out the room nightly in the middle of winter. It's not going to work at all. Yes, that's a warning, and that warning is just for starters."

The pages remained annoyingly blank. Still, I kept turning, breathing deeply to keep myself focused and patient. Somewhere in the middle of the grimoire, I saw ink begin to form. I held my breath as I turned the page, watching the letters come to life in front of my eyes.

The ink was a faded brown, and the cursive was lovely, and beautiful. The handwriting of someone genteel and for whom writing was a pleasure. A privilege. I looked at the date. The lines of writing blurred for a moment. I shook my head, and my vision cleared.

1782. This had been written over two hundred years ago. It was by far the oldest entry I'd seen.

The would-be goddess and the bull visited me again this evening. The woman is determined to be an Oracle. I do not understand. She is without a doubt the most oblivious woman I've ever met. She cannot—or will not—accept that unless one is chosen, one cannot have the armband. It is not there for the taking. Unfortunately, even after all these centuries, there are those who feel the gift of the Oracle merely need to be obtained. Thankfully, we can protect ourselves but I find this constant barrage from the unaware tiresome. I know that many feel if one does not do well with one's first consultant, one is doomed. But that is not the case. I have yet to solve the mystery my first consultant brought to me. There is no solving this particular question. I did, however, speak with Bettina's shade, and she told me to go out into the forest and accept the Oracle regardless of my failure. I did, and I have had four consultants since that time. My first still seeks my help, and I am saddened that I cannot solve that which he so desperately seeks. It is why I cannot send him away. But the would-be goddess has no more chance of removing the armband and taking up the Oracle than I do of becoming a man, heaven forfend. She has cast a spell upon me, and I believe that it —

Here the writing trailed off, as though the author fell asleep in the middle of the sentence. There were smudges along the bottom third of the page, and the lower corner was torn away, but nothing further.

So Ariadne had cast a spell. And it put this Oracle— what was her name?—I checked, and there was no name. Maybe something would appear later that would tell me who the Oracle was in 1782. The Oracle before the woman who wrote this was maybe Bettina?

At least, that was my thought. She'd mentioned speaking with Bettina's shade. I like the word. That was what Florry was. A shade.

I closed the grimoire, and leaned back against the headboard, thinking. She'd cast magic, but what would it do? I needed to talk to Florry, but she wasn't around. Or wasn't talking. Either way, it amounted to the same thing. Me not knowing what the hell I was dealing with. The idea that I was carting around a spell that I couldn't see, feel, or have any information about made me feel itchy, like that spot between your shoulder blades you can't reach.

I sighed. Well, when had anything been different with this Oracle gig? Everything I discovered, I had to find out on my own. And, I noted, I didn't discover a darn thing unless I went looking for it.

I tossed back the blankets and went to shower again. Time to get the day going. First things first—with all the focused burning I'd been doing to try to help Logan in the past two weeks, I was low on my supply of herbs. I needed to get over to the apothecary and replenish. I hadn't come across another consultant yet, but if Logan was any indication, I'd need to have a ready supply of the mixture.

As I got dressed, I thought about Nayla, the woman who had initially helped me. I hoped she'd be there. If not, I still had the list of herbs. I wanted to be prepared—how much could I buy in bulk, I wondered? How much could I buy without having Nayla or anyone else ask questions?

Such was life in a small town. Oak Bluffs was definitely a small town, even if I didn't live on an island.

I drove to the apothecary, a chime announcing my presence as I came in.

"Just a tick!" a voice called out from the back.

When I reached the counter in the back of the store, I waited.

"How can I help you?" Nayla came out from behind a curtain in the back, smiling. Her smile broadened as she saw me. "Oh, hey! Hi! You're back! Do you need more of the herbs already?" The questions were written all over her face.

I nodded. "Yes, I've been doing a lot of work on learning how to focus with my meditation, to quiet my thoughts." Laughing, to seem casual, I continued, "And I've gone through a lot of what you put together for me. I actually set some of it on fire," I said, laughing sheepishly this time. "So I need to order some more. Do you do bulk orders?"

Nayla looked at me for a moment. "We can, yes. How much do you need?"

I'd done some calculations based on what she sold me before, and I slid over the notepaper with what I wanted.

Nayla took it, and her eyebrows disappearing beneath her bangs. "That is definitely what I'd call a bulk order." She glanced up at me. "How soon do you need it?"

"As soon as you can put it together," I said, smiling like this was nothing out of the ordinary. Which was tough—it felt all kinds of awkward and weird to me. I felt like I was some kind of suspect, even though my mind knew I wasn't.

Accepting the gift of the Oracle and feeling comfortable in my new skin were two different things, apparently.

"It's going to take me a couple of days. Can you wait that long?" Nayla asked.

"Sure. I'll leave my address and number. Just call me when it's ready," I beamed at her as I left her my information.

As I drove home, my cell phone rang. I didn't answer it, as the number came up as Restricted. What did that mean? I didn't know anyone who wouldn't show up on caller ID. They could leave a message if it was important.

I turned my thoughts back to thinking about being the Oracle. There was so much I didn't know, and I felt the strength of my ignorance every time I turned around. But doing something, something that I knew I could use to help me—that made the lack of knowledge sting a little less.

When I came in the house, the smell of coffee was in the air, and Logan, his back to me, was in the kitchen. He spoke without turning around. "Hey, Wynter. Want some coffee?"

It didn't feel odd, or strange, to walk into my house and see a man in the kitchen. That was something I needed to consider—but maybe not right this instant. For the moment, I was going to be glad that he was here. He made me feel safer against all the things I still didn't know about my new life.

"Yes, please," I said, tossing my bag onto the island. I slid into one of the barstools. "How was your trip?"

He'd been looking into how to break into the details of his—Evander's—Swiss bank accounts. According to

Logan, you couldn't just hack into such an account and empty it. Unless you had all the login credentials, the accounts would lock. The Swiss banks didn't care if they were ever unlocked again. People paid for the level of security they provided. Apparently, so had Evander Thane. Additionally, Logan had gone to 529 Van der Veer Drive in Old Forge, a small hamlet in upstate New York, to the house that was in my dreams, to check it out. I couldn't deny that my heart leapt—in a good way—when I saw him in my kitchen. I'd been worried about him.

"Van der Veer is locked down like Fort Knox," he said. "And no one at the gate, no one in the little town, no one at all is talking. Whoever I was as Evander Thane, I must have been tossing money around like it was no big deal. No one has seen him, no one knows him all that well, but he's good to the town, even though Mr. Thane travels a great deal—" here his voice went up higher in an imitation of someone he'd met, "In short, Mr. Thane is none of our business, and none of mine either. He'll be here when he's here, and I need to move along." He grinned.

"You sure that's why they're not talking?" I asked.

Logan turned then, coffee cups in hand. His face was tired. He nodded. "I know the signs of a person well paid."

"The more I learn about you," I said as I spooned sugar into my cup, and then added creamer, "The more I worry."

He grinned again, his white teeth flashing against the sun warmed hue of his skin. "Well, I'm no angel."

I laughed. "No, I get that impression. I'm surprised no one recognized you."

"I didn't look exactly like myself," Logan said, brushing off my comment. "What animal did you have in here?" he asked, changing the subject abruptly.

I told him about Ariadne, and the bull, and how I thought there might have been a spell cast on me.

Logan frowned. "That's not good. What does your mentor say?"

I sighed. "Nothing. She's not talking to me right now?"

"Personal problems?" Logan asked, struggling to keep his face neutral.

"No, just not showing up. She's not on the clock or anything," I replied. "I wish she was, but that's not the case." I couldn't help the peevishness in my voice.

"Well, if you'd like to take your mind off your own issues, I could use some help," Logan said.

"Maybe. What are you proposing?"

"I want to go see the officer who is in charge of Evander's missing person report," Logan said, his expression serious now. "I want to know who filed it, and anything they've learned."

Thinking of Evander Thane, I gasped. "Oh, I have to tell you something!" I told him about seeing Davina, the cool blonde from my dream who had hung on Evander, at my doctor's office yesterday.

Logan's face darkened. "That's not a good thing, I don't think."

"No, I don't think so either. This is a small island. I've never seen her before. I mean, she could just be visiting, but…" I let my voice trail off. "It just seems too coincidental to be an accident. And if people have seen you around," I shrugged. "Well, it's not like you blend into the crowd."

"Is that a compliment?" Logan's eyes twinkled.

I felt like there was more being said than just words, but I couldn't puzzle that out right now. "You're good looking. You know that," I gave him what my kids called the 'mom look'. "Stop fishing for compliments. Davina being here—it just didn't feel right."

"Did she see you?"

"If she did, I didn't register," I said, remembering her disdainful gaze.

"That's a good thing. Well, with her, and the bull lady —maybe a trip is a good thing for you right now, Oracle."

"Convenient for you, too," I said.

"Absolutely," Logan laughed then. "I'll take it with no regrets."

"All right," I said. "Can I eat lunch first?"

"Of course. I'm not a monster," Logan replied, a mocking tone in his voice. "You might want to pack a bag, since we'll be staying overnight. It's a long trip. Unless there's a need to rush back?"

The thought of staying overnight somewhere other than my home with Logan made my insides leap in a way that I hadn't really expected, although given that I tamped down even my memories of him standing in my kitchen without a shirt, or in my room wrapped in a blanket every time they popped into my head, maybe I should expect it.

He really was a handsome man. And a funny man. And… I shook my head.

"Is that a no?" Logan asked.

"What? Oh, no, I mean, yes. I'm just thinking to myself," I said, feeling my cheeks get hot. Damn it. Get it together, I scolded myself. "I don't have anything on my schedule."

"I have a place we can stay if we need to. The missing person's report was filed in New York city, which is also strange," Logan frowned again. "I would have thought it would be in the hamlet where the house is in Old Forge, but..." he shrugged. "When I checked in the Old Forge police station, they directed me to a detective in Missing Persons in New York, and wouldn't tell me why it was sent there." He frowned, his fingers drumming on the island.

"And you're sure this is better than calling the detective in charge?" I asked.

"I do better with face to face," Logan said.

I could see that. More than I wanted to. "All right. After lunch. Once I eat, I'll go pack."

"I'll even make lunch, since you're taking the time to still help me," he said.

"It's nothing," I said.

"Well, he still owes you a service," I heard behind me.

CHAPTER THREE

"Where have you been?" I whirled around, seeing Florry leaning against the back of my couch, a cigarette in hand. She was in a white floral nightie with a green housecoat over the nightie, and canary yellow fluffy slippers. "You're going to have to help me with that whole... thing." I was conscious of Logan still here, listening. "I don't even know how to make a decision about... that." I still hadn't gotten used to her popping into my house.

I eyed Florry once more. When I passed on, I hoped I got this level of wardrobe choices. "Are those your own clothes?" I asked before I could stop myself.

Florry looked down. "What? Oh, yeah. When you go, you come back as you were in real life."

"And you lived in that in real life?" I asked incredulously.

"Sure. Why not? Super comfortable. No one ever suspects someone who looks like me of anything strange or out of the ordinary. Same with you, minivan soccer mom."

"I don't own a minivan," I said, stung.

"But you look like you could," Florry grinned.

"Wynter?" Logan asked from the other side of the island. He was looking at me and around the room. I guess he hadn't been around when Florry and I were so chatty.

"Mentor," I said, waving my hand at him. I found that I didn't want to talk to her with him so close. "I'm going to pack now, and then I'll come down and eat whatever culinary delight you whip up for us." I moved toward the stairs. "Can you be bothered to hang around and talk?" I asked Florry as I started up the stairway.

"Why do you think I'm here?" She rolled her eyes.

"Me?" Logan asked.

"Not everything's about you, cat man," Florry groused.

"No," I said to Logan. "I'll be down in a bit." I went upstairs. Once in my room, I closed the door. "Okay, what is the deal with that Ariadne? She showed up last night, and Goldie thinks she cast a spell on me."

Florry appeared, still looking all fresh and spring like in green, but sans cigarette. "Grimoire say anything?"

"An entry, two hundred years ago, about how Ariadne did the same thing to the Oracle at the time. But the entry wasn't complete. Goldie told me to take a shower."

"You notice anything different? Anything that would give you an idea about what sort of spell, or hex?" Florry was next to me as I walked into the closet to grab a couple of outfits. It was only overnight, but... I wanted to have choices. Why I might want those was something I didn't want to think about.

"I felt weird, like someone had dumped something on me." Glancing over, I could see that she was thinking, her lips pursed. "Whatever it was, it didn't wash off, but it's not as strong as when Ariadne cast the spell. I wish I knew what it was."

"She's a pain, that's for sure. I never saw her but the once, and after I cussed her out, she didn't come back. What did the entry say?" Florry's lips were thin as she spoke.

I left the closet and pulled the grimoire from under my pillow, hoping the entry was still there. It was, and I read it aloud to Florry.

"I don't know, Wynter, and I wish I could tell you more. I can ask the other girls, see what they know."

"This one, this Oracle—I think Bettina was her Florry," I said. "The date on the entry is 1782."

Florry nodded. "That helps. I'll see what I can find for you."

"Please do. It makes me nervous to think I'm walking around with a spell on me that I can't even feel, and probably won't notice until the worst possible time," I said.

"That's usually when spells show themselves," Florry laughed.

"Glad this is so amusing. I'll remember that when the mystery spell is hitting me," I said. "But have your laughs. I have something else I want to talk about."

"Shoot."

"What is my magic? I got rid of the blond necromancer guy who wanted the armband, I guess by thinking him away, but is that it? Is that all I have to do?"

"Could be. I'd tell you to practice on cat boy down there, sending him to and fro, but you might lose him. I don't think you want that," she grinned at me. "You get another consultant yet?"

"No and don't change the subject. I need to know more. If this is what I can do, this is great," I said, feeling a surge of excitement. "I want to know how to control it. That way, I know where I'm sending some-one, or at least trying to send them." I ignored the heat that rose into my face at Florry's teasing about Logan. This was more important. If someone came after me, I could just send them away. I could defend myself.

Although there was a problem about where they went, but if they were coming after me, they deserved what they got. That was easier to let go of than I thought. But after seeing the scary blond guy, and remembering how scared I was when he approached me, both in the grocery store and then in my house—I wasn't going to feel guilty if I sent someone to a place that was less than pleasant. Not that I wanted to kill anyone—not at all. In fact, the feeling I remembered when I cast him away from my home was one of power, and surety, and confidence in me and my ability, even as it scared the daylights out of me.

It had felt good. Better than good.

I wanted to feel that again. Although I could do without someone coming after me.

"So you're still hanging around with cat boy," Florry said. "He's easy on the eyes. I'd let him hang around, too."

"Stop," I said as I pulled out my small weekender bag. "How do I find out more about my magic? I feel like this is something I need to practice."

Florry tapped her lip. "Maybe practice sending something away and then bringing it back. That way, you can see if you can manage some kind of control."

"Like a flower pot," I mused.

"Exactly. A flower pot," Florry said. "Something that you won't have a hissy about losing."

"Definitely not a person," I said. "That's all you have for me? Practice?"

She shrugged. "All of us have different strengths, Wynter. No Oracle is the same. It's one of the things that is good about us."

"Meaning?" I looked at her.

"Meaning we're not cookie cutter. If we're all different, if we all have different skills, outside of the general Oracle responsibilities, then it's harder for those with ill intent to use us." Florry frowned. "And trust me, while it's more civilized in some ways now, it just means those with ill intent have gotten sneakier. So don't talk about your skills, or what you can do."

"Shelly and Logan know."

"Then keep it to them, and don't tell anyone else," Florry said sharply. "The less who know, the better. No one else was in here when you sent the nasty bad guy to somewhere else?"

I shook my head. "No. It was just me. I was scared to death. There was no way I'd stand a chance against someone like that."

"You need to change that way of thinking toot sweet," Florry said. "You always stand a chance. Just because you won't win in a hand to hand fight with someone doesn't mean you have no chance. Start practicing sending flower pots, like now."

"What was your magic?" I asked.

"I could tell when someone was lying. I could see the truth behind their words, like someone was writing it out on a blackboard in front of me." Her response was quick. "As they spoke, it was clear whether they were telling the truth or not."

"That's really cool," I said.

"It was handy. But your skill is as well. I know that you worry about safety. This is a good way for you to make yourself feel safe. So get to practicing." She nodded once.

"Well, I'm going to New York with Logan today," I said.

"Why? You found his past. Why are you still helping him?"

"No one else has come by looking for help," I shot back. "And I like Logan. He could have taken advantage of me, of how new I am. He didn't."

"Uh huh," Florry said, rolling her eyes. "Tell that to someone else, my girl."

I glared. "That's it."

"He has no business pulling you into whatever crap hole he's neck deep in," Florry snapped. "You have enough crap of your own."

I burst out laughing, even as I was annoyed. "That's true, but someone else's crap is always easier to handle."

"You can't," she said. "Your job is to be the Oracle. Not cat boy's fixer."

"Stop," I said. "Once I have another consultant, Logan is on his own."

"You gonna kick him out?"

"I don't know," I said, feeling defensive.

"Uh, huh. I'm not blind," Florry said.

"Will you stop? There's nothing going on between us. Nor will there be. I'm a widow, and—"

"You keep telling yourself that, toots. Anyway. Take the grimoire. You don't want to leave it lying around. And don't let him drag you further into his problems." She began to fade.

A thought hit me. "Florry, wait!"

She appeared again, frowning. "What?"

"Do you want me to talk to your friend?"

"What are you talking about?"

"Caro," I said. I'd been meaning to talk to her about this, because I'd been thinking about the woman who had lost her friend. "You said that Caro was like your helper. Was she with you when you faded?"

A flash of pain crossed Florry's face. It was stark, and it hit me as though it were my own.

"Caro was the best friend I ever had," Florry said, her voice quiet. "I don't know if she was with me. I don't remember what happened. Just... I woke up, although I didn't remember going to sleep, and I was in between." She frowned.

A maelstrom of emotion swirled around me. Caro had been important to Florry. I could feel it radiating from my mentor. Hell, it was almost drowning me. But Florry's expression had gone neutral.

Interesting.

"Do you want me to go and see her? Or call her?"

"I don't know," Florry said. "Can I get back to you?"

"Of course," I said.

She nodded. "'K. See ya, girlie. Behave in the big city." She disappeared.

I stared. There was more here than met the eye. I made a mental note to look up a Caro or Caroline in Lost Chance, Kansas, and see if she was still there. I stopped my thought process. It wasn't Lost Chance. Florry and I had talked about the little house where I'd first met her, when I'd been drawn to the grimoire. What was it? I thought hard. Not Lost Chance. Lost Springs. That was the name. Lost Springs, Kansas. From what I'd seen, what I remembered of sitting on the small porch, looking out across a field—there wasn't much there.

A knock on my door made me jump. "Yes?"

"Lunch is ready," Logan said from behind the door.

"That's great, thank you," I replied. "I'll be down in a few."

"All right," he said.

I heard footsteps walking away. Had he been listening while I spoke with Florry? He couldn't hear her, but he could figure things out from my side of the conversation. I shook my head. What was I thinking? I trusted Logan.

He'd given me no reason not to. Florry's warnings aside, I decided that I'd continue to trust him until he gave me a reason to stop. Even a small reason— because I didn't think that Florry was completely bonkers.

I finished packing, and when I went back downstairs, Logan was putting together tuna fish sandwiches.

They were delicious. I wondered if that was because it was food I didn't have to make.

"I'll drive," Logan said as we were eating. "It's the least I can do."

I nodded, Florry's warnings still ringing in my ears, despite my efforts to dispel them. "Can you promise me you won't expose me unnecessarily?" I asked. "To danger, or anything like that?"

Logan paused with his sandwich halfway to his mouth. "Of course. I know that you're doing more for me than any obligation. And we're friends. At least, I think we are." He watched me for a moment. "What's wrong?" he asked.

"I'm just worried. I need to be able to protect myself, and at the moment, I don't feel that I have any good ideas on how to do it."

"Well, your pepper spray game is ace," he said. "Carry your Taser as well. You also have some magic," he added.

"The magic isn't a sure thing," I said, waving it off. I didn't want to make a big deal of it. Better he think that I didn't rely on it. Which at the moment was one hundred percent true. But I would be practicing, and if those who knew about my magic thought I sucked at it —all the better.

"I won't let any harm come to you. You have my word," Logan said solemnly.

"Thank you," I said.

When we finished, Logan cleaned up while I took a walk around the house, making sure things were locked, and that nothing would go awry if I was gone for a night.

"Ready?" he asked when I came back down into the living room. "You have everything?" He eyed my bag.

Not only did I have a couple of changes of clothes, but the grimoire was buried at the bottom of the bag. I wasn't letting it out of my sight. Which would mean I'd need to get a bigger purse when I wanted to carry it around during the day. Or when I had to. Yet another thing on the 'to do' list. "Let's go," I said.

CHAPTER FOUR

I was surprised when Logan pulled into the ferry depot. "We're taking the ferry?" I asked.

He nodded. "I like the ferry. A lot less stressful than driving."

"Logan, this is—" I was about to protest. This was ridiculously expensive.

He held up a hand. "You're helping me. Don't worry about it, Wynter. I would do this whether you were with me or not."

I let it be.

I'd never taken the ferry to New York, and the cata-maran was definitely upscale. Logan got us some bottled water, and we found seats on the upper deck. "You're right," I said, as we sat down. "This is much nicer than driving."

"We have to take a ferry anyway," he shrugged. "And I hate driving in New York."

"It's strange that the report was filed there," I said, thinking about what he'd told me about Evander's missing person report.

"Nothing about this is normal," Logan said. His green eyes darkened, taking on a golden glow. I wondered if this was his panther considering making an appearance, or if this was what happened when he was angry.

"How is it going with hacking the accounts?" I lowered my voice. What with the kids and I traveling to Arizona, Logan and I hadn't had much of a chance to speak. My kids had been in and out of the house more in the lead up to our trip, as well as when we'd returned, which meant he'd had to go over to Shelly's more, although Shelly didn't mind a bit. I didn't want the questions a man who looked like Logan would bring. Not from anyone, and certainly not from my kids. Florry and her insinuation was bad enough.

Not to mention, the glimpses I'd had of Logan with his shirt off didn't help. I was trying to keep things professional. No matter where my mind wandered.

"I think my guy is almost there," Logan said. "It's not actually hacking the account, but the information to access the account. If we hack it, it will lock everything down, which defeats the purpose. I need to be able to get into it as well as move things around." He sighed. "I also need to keep things low key to not raise any alarms. If all activity stopped when I landed in the desert, there's been no activity for seven years."

"Makes sense," I said. "Any idea what Evander was doing? Why all the people I kept seeing in my dream were all wanting something from him, or wanting to get something over on him?"

"I don't think I was a good guy," Logan said. "I'm shady now, but I have standards. I don't know that Evander had the same standards." His shoulders bunched. "It's not pretty, what I've found out. Evander was shady as hell. And there are rumors that he—I— am not completely human."

"Well, you're not," I said.

"I mean outside the panther," Logan said.

"What are you?" I asked. "Or what do the rumors think you are? As Evander, I mean?"

He shrugged, although his shoulders didn't fully relax. "A mage. A necromancer. Someone who stood in the crossroads and made a deal with a devil, if not Lucifer himself."

I laughed.

He didn't.

"Seriously?" I asked. "These are real things?"

"Welcome to a whole new world, Ms. Chastain," Logan smiled, but it wasn't a smile of happiness. Normally, he looked far younger than me, but today, right now, he looked much, much older.

"Do you want to talk about it?" I asked.

"No." He spoke quickly.

"All right." I changed the subject. We talked about the visit to Arizona, which he was very interested in.

"I don't know if I could be as easy about this as you are," Logan said, leaning back and gazing across the water's horizon.

"I'm not easy," I sighed. "But I can't throw a hissy in front of the kids."

"Why not?" He looked over.

"Because I'm the adult," I said.

"Aren't they adults?" Logan asked. "It's not like they're little kids."

I sighed. "That's not it. It's just——"

"What?"

"Derek is gone. Yes, he screwed up. Yes, I've had to make changes. Yes, I'd like to drop kick him into the sun. But in light of how my life is changing..." It was my turn to shrug and look out over the water.

I met Logan's eyes again. "This just doesn't feel like something I want to put a lot of energy into. And I don't want it to hang over my kids. They don't deserve this. Besides, she's a nice woman, and her kids are darling." I laughed, thinking about Nathan mentioning no poison. "It's making it easier for my kids to live their lives without getting caught up in something that can't be changed."

"That's very forgiving," Logan said.

"Well, Derek isn't here. I might not be as forgiving if I had to look at him," I said, in total honesty.

"Do you miss him?"

I shook my head without even thinking about it. "I miss the man I thought I knew. I didn't really know him—I didn't know the man that could hurt two families like this, who could justify this whole mess," I waved a hand to encompass all my personal drama, "And still come home to both families. It's weird. My friends are angrier than I am. They think I'm in shock, and I'm going to completely drop the plot at some point."

"Then they don't know you very well, do they?" he said, grinning.

"Well—" I stopped, my blood running cold as I looked over Logan's shoulder. Holy. Hello.

"What?" Logan tensed, watching my face intently.

"You need to turn toward me, and not face outward," I said. "Like, don't look around, face the wall behind me, and don't talk or laugh too loud."

Logan carefully turned his body, stretching an arm behind me along my seat. His face was blank, his eyes darting back and forth. "What do you see?"

I liked that he didn't swivel around, asking me what was I talking about. Although it did suggest that he was far more used to being in danger than I was.

"Remember I told you I saw the blonde from my dream at my doctor's office yesterday? Davina?" I asked, my lips barely moving.

"Yes, but talk normally. No one else can hear us with all the noise out here. You look like someone's holding a gun to you. That will attract more attention than anything I might do."

I didn't move, my eyes glued to the blonde on the other side of the deck.

"Wynter." Logan's voice was gentle. "Look at me."

It was an effort to tear my eyes away from her, but I managed.

"Relax and tell me what you see. Smile while you're talking."

"She's here. Davina. The cold blonde, the one from all my dreams, or visions," I said. "She's on our damn ferry, Logan! What if she sees you? She'll know who you are, know that you're not dead—"

Logan leaned close to me, and I could smell his warmth, his spicy scent. "Take a deep breath. There's no need to panic. People see what they want to. She's not expecting to see Evander Thane in jeans, or worn flannel and even more worn work boots. My hair is longer, and I'm not Evander."

I blinked, focusing on breathing in and out. Something about this woman made my heart race. She was dangerous. I'd sensed that even in my dreams. Florry and Goldie told me to listen to my instincts, and they were screaming warnings as though a hurricane was coming.

Davina was leaning on the rail, her hands clasped in front of her, her long hair streaming with the wind. She was turned slightly so that I could see her profile, and she almost looked like she was smiling. Large, rounded sunglasses covered half her face, but I'd just seen her—there was no mistaking who it was.

Then her lips curved into a wide smile, and I saw her hold out a hand. A man in slacks and a coat with a dress shirt open at the neck and no tie came closer and took it, bringing her palm to his mouth to kiss it, all while watching her.

Davina smiled even more widely. It reminded me of a shark. She laughed, although I couldn't hear it. The man came closer to her, and she looked down, maybe trying for some kind of demure look.

"She is just all about reeling them in," I said before I could stop myself.

Logan laughed quietly. "That is positively catty, Wynter." He risked a glance over his shoulder, watching her for a moment. "That's the woman I was close to?"

"Yes," I said.

He was silent, just watching as she flirted with the man next to her. "I don't see it. She's very obvious." He turned to face me again. "There is no way she'll recognize me," he said. "I'm not anywhere near the class of man she likes."

"Go ahead, brush off my concern," I snapped. "But my warning signs are screaming bloody murder."

"I didn't say I was going to ignore your concern. If you tell me I need to make sure she doesn't see me, I'm going to listen. You've been right so far. I'm just trying to get a sense of who I used to be." He shook his head. "I don't see anything of the man I am now in the man I was."

I opened my mouth to reply when a flash of light blinded me, and I was in a darkened, cool space, nowhere near the sunny day on the water I'd just been in.

Looking around, it felt like I was underwater. I could feel movement—a lot of it—around me, but it was all things I couldn't see. Cool and green, with constant danger lurking in the background. Oddly, I wasn't afraid. I knew that the danger wasn't targeted or focused toward me. I knew that I was safe. How I knew, I had no idea.

"Hello?" I said.

Daughter, you are here once more. I find that I am enjoying this, a deep voice said, one that resonated through my very bones.

"Tethys?" I asked.

Yes, daughter. I am here to deliver a message.

"What is it?" I asked, looking around the cool darkness. There was no one visible, although I could feel life all around.

I have felt your power. It is like mine, out of the wild darkness, untamed. It has yet to fully show itself, but it's there.

"Oh," I said. I didn't like the sound of that. Her words rang within me, though—something Logan had said. What was it? That I was on the verge of power? That was it. When I asked him if he thought I was weak, and he said that he sensed a lot of power in me.

Well. Here was another magical being, one a lot more powerful than I'd ever be, telling me the same thing.

Maybe it was time to listen.

Tethys deep tones brought me back to my present surroundings. *You will need to bring your powers to heel, because otherwise, they may rage out of control.*

"I don't know how!" I said, my voice rising to a shout, letting the fear her words brought on overwhelm me.

Trust your instincts. You have the power of space, of moving space. Like the ocean, space is everywhere.

"What does that mean?" I asked, feeling my heart beating madly in my chest. Her words brought no comfort.

It means that you are strong, should you choose to be. And remember what we spoke of before. All is eventually revealed. The ocean may take, but eventually, she always returns that which has been taken.

"Who is the message from?" I asked.

From me. I feel your power, and I sense your desire to master it, to conquer the fear it brings. You have the strength. You need to use it.

"Is this going to be normal, you and me chatting when I'm on the ferry?" I asked.

I felt rather than heard a deep, rolling chuckle. *Perhaps. I haven't been interested in the doings of humans for many moons. But I find you interesting, little daughter. There is much magic, much power, that is moving about you. It is driven by you. You are tied to the sea in some manner, which means you are tied to me. I have not seen a human draw this much magic around themselves in a long time. The time is coming when you will need to make a choice. Be prepared.*

"I already made my choice!" I shouted. I could feel her presence moving away. "What else do I need to choose?"

Be prepared, daughter. Her voice faded.

I blinked, seeing the darkness fade, the greenish gloom around me lift. Then I blinked again, and Logan was peering down at me, his eyes worried.

"Wynter?" he hissed. "Wake up!"

"I'm awake," I said.

"What happened?"

"A trance," I said. "I got a message. Not about you, at least I don't think so."

Logan sat back, his arm still across the back of my seat. I was glad to see that he still had his back to where Davina and the man stood at the railing. Neither were looking at us, completely absorbed in one another.

"Did I make a lot of noise?" I asked.

Logan shook his head. "No, you leaned back against the wall—" We were sitting in a pair of seats tucked into a small alcove around the cabin— "and your eyes fluttered. I held onto you so you didn't face plant out of the seat or anything. But you didn't speak, and your eyelids kept fluttering while your head moved back and forth."

He removed his hands from my waist. I found that I was sorry to lose the feel of them. No, I thought. No. I'm not going to think about this. We're friends. Just friends. That mantra didn't resonate with the imprint his hands left on me, unfortunately.

"I'm sorry if it was alarming," I said. "I find this alarming myself. I'm okay," I added. "Although I need some water." I brought the bottle to my mouth and drank the rest of the bottle.

"What happened?" Logan asked again.

I waved a hand. "It's Oracle related. Not Logan related. Or even Wynter related," I added, smiling.

Logan didn't return the smile. "Are you sure?"

"No," I said as I turned to look out over the water. "I'm not sure about a lot at the moment. Can you distract me? What is it you plan to do with this detective? What do you think he or she can tell you?" I didn't want to talk about Tethys. Or anything else related to me.

Logan slowly blinked. I got the impression he saw right through my clumsy attempt to change the subject. He didn't push me, however, and leaned back. "I want to know who filed it. Who is the contact should the detective find anything? When was it filed? Seven years ago? Longer?"

"Again, why is it you think you couldn't email or call?" I asked.

"Because people often tell you more when they have to look at you," he grinned, and I could almost see the fangs of his panther at the corners of the grin. "And I enjoy a boat ride."

I laughed then. "It is nice," I said. "I've never done this before."

"How can you call yourself a local?" Logan put a hand to his heart.

"This is one of the tourist things," I said, feeling smug.

"Call me a tourist then," Logan said. "No need to get snotty."

"Oh, I'll be as snotty as I want. I'm a native," I said.

"Which means what?" Logan asked.

"I was born here. My mom couldn't get off island fast enough to make it to the hospital, so I was born in the master bedroom of the house. Not many people are born here," I said.

Logan didn't speak, doing a little gazing over the water himself. "Didn't you ever want to go anywhere else?"

"I had a husband who was a pilot. We traveled during his off season because he wanted the kids to see more than just the island. All my kids left for school and don't have plans to come back. But I love it here. I love the sound of the sea. I love the mood of the ocean, how it changes. Some people can't wait to get away. I've never wanted to leave," I finished. Tethys said I was connected to the sea, and she called me daughter. I was, I realized. I couldn't imagine living away from it.

"I can't remember feeling that way about anywhere," Logan said.

"My kids think I'm a complete weirdo. I love small island life. I like that we fight like cats and dogs over turning our intersection into a roundabout," I laughed, thinking of the fighting over The Blinker intersection. "I like that we use the word 'Beetlebung' in normal conversation."

"And now all the people here are giving you the side eye," Logan frowned, remembering an earlier conversation we'd had.

I laughed again. "Oh, you mean because of the woman who owns the hotel?" Hazel Babbington had been angry at me since Ash disappeared from her B&B. She got even angrier when I told her that her security sucked.

He nodded.

"Shelly took care of that. She's on a local committee with Hazel, and when Hazel started her trash talk, Shelly asked why Hazel wasn't at the desk, why no one was at the desk. Then she asked if there were more guests that had disappeared and wondered if Hazel had just packed up their belongings and quietly moved them to the lost and found." I pealed with laughter. "I would have given a lot to see the old bat's face."

"Shelly plays dirty," Logan snickered.

"You've already seen that. It's not a surprise. She believes in being fair, and Hazel is an old bag who definitely doesn't play fair. People are still gossiping, but it's calmed down. It doesn't matter," I shook my head a little, and found that I meant what I said. Before, I'd been hurt at how ready some in the town were to believe the worst of me. But now, I didn't care. I wasn't going anywhere. No one was going to try to make me leave. There would be no burning of the witch, or the

Oracle, in the town square. They'd have to just learn to live with it.

Thankfully, Logan didn't ask anything more about my vision. I trusted him, but I didn't want to share. We talked about what he remembered after being found in the desert, and he talked about his friend Mark, the shifter who had found him, and nursed him back to health. Mark had also helped Logan to find a way to make a living, and I could see the genuine affection Logan had for the man.

"I may ask him to come out here," Logan said almost to himself. "He's a good guy to have around." He stopped, looking down at me. "Not that he would need to stay with you. In fact, if I'm going to be here for a while, I need to find my own place to live."

"You might want to get moving if that's your plan," I said. "It's almost summer. There won't be anywhere to rent. Not that I'm booting you out, but if you want your own place, there's not a lot of time to secure a rental."

He nodded, not speaking.

I peered around him. "She's gone," I said. "They both are."

Logan turned then to look where Davina had been standing with the man. "It's a little too coincidental," he said.

"My thoughts exactly."

"Well, I'll sit up here and pull my hat down over my face," Logan said, pulling a weathered olive ball cap with faded writing on the front out of his back pocket, "If you'll grab us something more to drink and all the snacks they have."

"I hope they have enough," I said as I got up to go into the small concessions area. In the short time I'd known Logan, he ate enough for three men. Maybe four.

I came out twenty minutes later, having bought as many granola and nuts and cheese snacks that I could, hoping it would keep Logan somewhat full.

He grinned as he saw me come back with a large paper bag. "You weren't kidding."

"I've seen you when you get hangry," I said.

Logan laughed good-naturedly and dove into the bag. We ate in a companionable silence, and I allowed my eyes to close and enjoy the sun and the smell of the salt air. I thought about Tethys' message. What sort of choice would I need to make? I'd accepted the job of the Oracle. What more was there? After turning her words over and over in my mind, I had no more insight than when Tethys dragged me into wherever it was she dragged me. I put it aside. At the moment, this was not life or death, and it would keep.

At least, I hoped it would.

When the ferry approached New York, Logan pulled his phone out and arranged a car. To be on the safe side, we waited until we saw Davina and the man she was with leave the ferry. Davina tossed her creamy blonde hair in the wind, her arm twined through the man's.

"She's a hunter," Logan said.

"That's one way to put it," I replied.

"Well, now she's gone, so we can leave." There was a dark black car with tinted windows waiting alongside the dock, and a tall man held a sign that said 'Gentry'.

"Hello," Logan said. "Wynter, if you hop in, I'll tell him where we're going."

The tall man tucked the sign under his arm and practically leapt to open the back door. I slid into a dark car, cool with air conditioning, and dark leather all around.

Logan joined me a moment later. The car pulled away smoothly, and I allowed myself to lean back and relax.

"It will be about half an hour with traffic," Logan said. "Yet another reason not to drive. I'd be clawing at the steering wheel."

I smiled without looking over at him. I must have nodded off, because he was gently shaking my arm after what felt like only a moment later. I was sleepy, and I could tell that I'd gotten some sun on our trip over.

"We're nearly there," Logan said. "You ready?"

"What do you want me to do?" I asked.

"Just listen to him. Or her. Get a sense of what they're saying. Like, are they lying?" He ran his hand through his hair and then settled the ball cap back onto his head. "I'm going to say that we're friends of Evander, and we're concerned. We're looking for an update, if there are any."

"We're here sightseeing," I said.

He nodded. "Exactly."

"Where are we?" I asked.

"At the Manhattan South precinct, going to the Special Investigations Division to see Detective Kane."

"Well, good to know you have a name."

"For that, I did get someone to hack into the files. Most of the missing person stuff is general, with no details on who to call."

"Won't that make the detective suspicious?" I asked.

"Maybe," Logan shrugged, his expression unconcerned. "It's all right if he is."

The car slid to a stop.

"I'll need you to wait," Logan said. "Can you find parking?"

"I'll manage," the tall man said. He held up a card. "Call me when you're ready to leave."

"Thanks, man," Logan took the card, and the driver was out of the car to come around and open the door for me. He was fast. Almost too fast.

"Is he something special?" I hissed at Logan.

Logan didn't answer, but one side of his mouth quirked up. "Maybe."

"You need to tell me these things," I said.

"Okay, okay. I'm sorry."

I got out and Logan was out behind me. He lightly ran up the steps to the precinct and held the door open.

At the front desk, the officer gave us an appraising look. "Detective Kane isn't here," he said.

"This is one of his older cases," I leaned forward, letting my eyes widen. "We just want a few minutes of his time. Is there someone else we can speak with?"

"Do you have more information on the case?" the officer who looked to be only a few years older than Theo, asked.

"I don't know. We've never spoken to him, and no one has heard anything about Evander in so long," I let my eyes fall down to the desk between us.

There was a silence, and then the officer picked up a phone. "Detective Rochester? Arnold, front desk. There are a couple of people here with me who want to talk about one of your missing persons cases, one with Kane." He stopped, listening. "Okay, yes sir." He nodded a few more times and then hung up the phone. "He'll be right out. If you'd like to have a seat," he indicated a pair of benches that were worn looking in the foyer.

"Thank you," I said, letting my smile beam at him.

The tops of his cheeks went pink. "Of course, ma'am. My pleasure." He looked down quickly.

We took a seat on the benches, which had discoloration all along them. I tried not to think about what could do that and stared ahead.

"Very good," Logan murmured into my ear. "The poor kid was about to swallow his tongue."

"I don't know what you're talking about," I said.

After ten minutes or so, a man with dark hair, in a shirt with rolled-up sleeves and a tie, and a harried expression came out from the area behind the front desk. He leaned over toward Arnold, the front desk officer.

Logan was looking down at his phone and didn't see the man.

I watched him look at the two of us, measuring us. If this wasn't Rochester, I'd eat one of Florry's slippers.

He met my eyes, and his chin lifted in acknowledgement. Two people, potentially adversaries, sizing each other up.

Things like this were why I preferred my island life.

He straightened his tie at his neck and came out from behind the desk.

"Hello, I'm Tate Rochester. Detective Kane, the detective assigned to the missing persons case you inquired about, isn't here. But I can help you," he said, his hand outstretched.

I got up faster than Logan and took Tate's hand. It was warm, and I could feel his worry, his suspicion, and his interest in us all at once.

What I didn't feel was something shady, like I'd felt with blond necromancer man from the moment I met him in the grocery store. This was a man who was dedicated to his job.

"I'm Wynter Chastain," I said. "Thank you for seeing us."

CHAPTER FIVE

*B*eside me Logan made a choking sound. It was lost as he tried to cover his outburst with a cough. I didn't turn to look at him, not wanting to be obvious, but I wondered what I'd said to make him choke like that. So much for being cool in front of the police.

"This is my friend, Logan Denford," I continued. While I didn't mind giving away my name, I wasn't going to give away Logan's. I had no idea why I did it —this wasn't my norm. But something told me to not tell anyone Logan's real name. I went with it.

"Good to meet you both," Rochester said. "Why don't we go back to a conference room where we can speak?" He walked to the front desk, taking a file and tucking it under his arm, and leading us off toward the right. We walked past the desks of people working, and then Rochester walked ahead and opened a door into a room with light green walls and a table and four chairs within.

"Please come in," he said.

I walked in first, followed by Logan. I sat down, Logan doing the same, but a lot more slowly.

"Can I get you something to drink?" Rochester asked.

"I'm fine," I said.

Logan shook his head.

"All right, great." Rochester closed the door and sat down opposite us. "Now, how can I help you?"

I leaned forward, clasping my hands in front of me. Minivan soccer mom, Florry had said. The sort that doesn't look suspicious at all. This man across from me looked like he would suspect me anyway if circumstances demanded, but I might as well start out as though I had no agenda other than finding out what happened to my friend Evander Thane.

Which was true, after a fact?

"It's been a number of years since the report was filed for poor Evander—" I began.

"Seven-and-a-half," Rochester said without looking at the file on the table.

"And we've called the Old Forge police department, such as it is," I said, "But no one can tell us anything."

"How do you know Evander Thane?" Rochester asked. His eyes narrowed slightly.

"We are business friends," I said. "Although I didn't see him after he had that wonderful party at his house to celebrate his last acquisition. How long was that before he went missing?" I turned to Logan, hoping he'd know.

"About a month," Logan said. He had his hat down low on his forehead. "Maybe more, five weeks?" He ended his words with a question.

"A little over five weeks," Detective Rochester said.

"We were so shocked," I shook my head.

"How did you get the contact information for this department?" Rochester asked. There was an edge in his voice.

"The nice man in Old Forge gave it to us. So strange that it wasn't filed with them, when that was where Evander lived."

"Why was the report filed with your department, Detective Rochester?" Logan asked, his voice quiet. "Old Forge is a long way from here."

"The last place Evander Thane was seen was in the city." Rochester flipped open the file, looking down at it for several seconds, although I'd bet he didn't need it. "He had dinner with friends and got into a cab. According to them, he was supposed to meet them for brunch, and never showed up. No one has seen him since." Tate Rochester looked up at first me, then Logan. He had the wide-eyed look I'd employed earlier. "I don't suppose you'd know anything about that?"

I shook my head. "Who filed the report, if you don't mind me asking, Detective?"

"A woman named Davina Lourdes," he said.

I started. Davina again. She kept popping up like mold in all of this.

"Tall, blonde, very cool and together?" Logan asked.

"Do you know her?" Rochester asked almost immediately. He directed his question to Logan, but he was watching me.

"We met her at the party," I said. "She was quite keen on Logan."

"Was he keen on her?" Rochester asked me.

"I don't know. He didn't brush her off, and he had no problem doing that," I said with a small laugh. "But he didn't seem to have the same level of interest that she did."

"Do you know who was with him the night he disappeared?" Logan asked.

"I do, but can you tell me why you're interested?"

I sighed. "We have to tell him, Logan," I said.

"Tell me what?" Rochester leaned forward.

"Well, I have known Evander since we were young. We did, in fact, do business with him, but our parents all moved in the same circles," I said. "Evander lived a much more elaborate life than I did as we got older. But he was a good friend," I smiled then, thinking of Logan. So far, he was a good friend. I wasn't lying. "And I didn't always care for the people who hung around him. He was quite well off," I added. "Although I'm sure you knew that."

"No heirs, either," Logan said. He added it as though I wasn't talking about something different.

"None that have come forward, no," Rochester nodded. "We've looked."

"He wasn't married, and there were no children," I said. "That I know of."

"And Davina Lourdes?" Rochester asked.

"Well, she liked him," I said, remembering the way she watched him, like a predator waiting for the moment to pounce on her prey. What had Logan called her? A hunter? He was spot on. I laughed again. "It's silly, but I didn't care for her much." I knew how that made me sound, and I was all right with it. It was true. I didn't care for Davina at all. "I'm worried, Detective Rochester. No one else seems interested in finding him. No one has seen him. His case is all the way down here, not where he lived. Has anyone come forward with any information?"

"No," Rochester said.

"Can you tell us who he had dinner with?" Logan asked again.

"Why do you want to know?"

"Because we might know them," I said.

"Forgive me, but you two don't seem the type to be close with the kind of people Evander Thane was with when he disappeared," Rochester said. This time, he was watching Logan carefully.

"Don't I know it," I said. "He's a far cry from the kid I jumped in mud puddles with."

That made Rochester smile the tiniest smile I'd ever seen. It was gone as fast as it had been there. "I can show you the list, and their pictures, if you like," he said, rifling through the file.

Something had made him decide to share.

He pulled out four pictures.

"Davina Lourdes," he said, turning it so we could see her. "Although she was Davina Thackery at the time."

"This is Charlene Neville," he pushed over a picture of the woman I'd seen at the party who'd also been competing for Evander's attention, only she'd been the one I thought of as the woman in blue.

"And her husband, Robert Neville," a picture of one of the men who had been with the small group around Evander at the party.

When had they gotten married? "That's interesting. I saw both of them at the party, and neither were acting married," I said. There had been no ring—well, no wedding ring, at least—on Charlene's hand.

"They got married about five years ago," Rochester said. He pushed another picture over.

I had to stifle my gasp, but it was too late. Rochester had seen my reaction, even as I tried to hide it.

The picture was of Tomas Severn, the creepy man I'd danced with and then hidden from in subsequent dreams. That was odd. I hadn't gotten the impression that he was all that close with Evander.

Then I remembered the conversation I'd had with Evander, before I'd run out of the dream.

"What brings you to this party this evening?" Logan-Evander asked. "As we haven't met, and we're celebrating my latest find this evening."

"A chance acquaintance," I said. "Tomas Severn," I added, remembering Tomas' last name just in time.

Logan-Evander looked up and beyond me. His eyes found Tomas, who was not looking over at us, and I saw the predatory way that Logan-Evander sized him up. Whatever else was going on, Logan-Evander was not impressed with poor Tomas.

I wondered if my mentioning Tomas to Evander at that moment in time had brought the blond man to Evander's attention. If so, Tomas was lucky. While Evander was shady, Tomas was creepy. He was not in the same class as Evander. Even with my small store of knowledge of the supernatural world, I could tell that.

"Do you know him?" Rochester asked.

"I spoke with him at the party. I'd never met him before. Tomas… what was his last name?" I turned to Logan.

"Savant?" Logan asked.

"No," I shook my head. "No, but that's close." I looked back to the detective. "What's his last name?"

"Severn. Tomas Severn." Tate Rochester was watching me carefully.

It reminded me of the way Davina had watched Evander in my vision, and the way she'd been focused on the man on the ferry.

Like prey.

Although I felt like the gazelle among the lions, or panthers, as it were, I wasn't scared. "That sounds right," I said. "I can't remember. It's been a long time. Odd. He didn't seem to know Evander very well."

"Is there anything else you can tell me?" Rochester asked.

"I went to Old Forge. The staff seems to think Evander will be back soon," Logan spoke suddenly.

"What?" I turned to him.

"What do you mean?" Rochester asked.

Logan shrugged. "I was passing by, and I stopped in to see if anything was known. The staff thinks he's coming back at some point. It's still staffed. Someone is paying them."

"That's an interesting point," Rochester asked. "Why do you care?"

"Because we miss our friend," I said carefully. I could tell that Rochester wasn't sure if he should keep talking or just arrest us and beat information out of us. At least, that's what he wanted to do.

As someone who was frequently looking for information that I didn't get, I could empathize. But I wasn't going to jail for anyone.

"What do you think happened?" Rochester sat back in his chair, the energy in the room shifting as he did so.

"I think one of his shady friends wanted something Evander had, and… " I stopped.

"And?"

"And they did something to him," I whispered. Again, this was true. Whoever had dumped him in the desert was personally invested in making sure that not only did he die, but that he suffered.

There was silence after I spoke.

"As it happens, I agree with you. I also find it interesting that no one has come looking for a man that so many were concerned for when he went missing," Rochester said, crossing his arms in front of him. "You're the first people who have come to inquire since the first year."

"What?" I asked. "No one else?"

Rochester shook his head. "Is there anything you can tell me? Anywhere he might go?"

"I don't know," I said. "We weren't close in the years before he disappeared. Much as I wished otherwise."

"I was surprised to find the house open, and fully staffed," Logan said. "I asked if anyone else was there, and they closed the door in my face."

"Really?" Rochester asked.

"Yes," Logan said. "Which is why we decided that when we were here, we'd come and talk to you. Because that's not normal, to have the house open, and things running as though he's there when he's not."

Rochester was nodding. "Are you making a formal request, Mr. Denford?"

"What are you saying?" I looked between the two men. I wanted to hear one of them say it out loud.

"What your friend is hinting at is that someone is taking advantage of Evander Thane's absence, and living in his home, as though Evander is still there. Why anyone would do that, I can't say. Perhaps I need to go and find out."

"No," I said, letting my eyes go wide once more. "You think someone is living there? Then yes, you need to go and see who it is and toss them out on their ear!" I sounded like my mother.

Which wasn't a good thing.

"Is there anything else you can tell me?" Rochester said.

"No," I said. "At least, I don't have anything. I wish I did. I was hoping you had something for us."

"I'm sorry, Ms. Chastain. I don't."

"Well," I stood up. "Then I will say thank you for allowing us to take up your time. I wonder, though, Detective, would you be so kind as to let me know what you discover, if anything?"

Tate Rochester stared at me for a moment and then nodded, his movement sparse and sharp. He gave me the impression that he moved quickly and without hesitation all the time. That he was always watching as he did so.

"Thank you," I said.

I wrote down my cell number, sliding it across to Rochester.

He got up and walked us out. At the desk, he stopped, leaning against the desk. "Thank you for coming in," he said.

Logan also leaned against the counter, his back to the door. I was standing between the two men, and I looked over my left shoulder. A man stood at the opposite side of the front desk, staring a hole into me. I tried to keep my expression the same. I had no idea if I succeeded. The man's stare was intense and even though I wasn't looking at him, I could feel it.

Logan turned then and saw the staring man. He inhaled deeply, and I heard his small gasp. He met the man's eyes. He turned me toward the exit, walking quickly. As we reached the door, Logan tucked my arm into his. "He's watching us. Don't turn around," he whispered.

"Why? Why all the stink eye and what do you smell?"

"Because. Just don't. Think sad thoughts." He pushed open the door and ushered me out. Once out on the sidewalk, he called the driver of the car.

I opened my mouth to speak, and he stopped me. "Not here," he said, his voice still low.

Once we were in the car, I turned to him. "What was that about with that other cop? And why did you let me do most of the talking?"

"Because Rochester liked you better than me," Logan said. "You did great, Mata Hari. You were practically batting your eyelashes at him."

"I was not," I made a shooing motion at him. "I was trying to look like the innocent childhood friend who was clinging to a relationship that really wasn't there anymore, and who was completely naïve."

Logan looked at me. His mouth opened to speak, then he closed it again, and shook his head, his fingers rubbing his eyes. His shoulders shook.

After a moment, I realized that he was laughing.

"What? Weren't we trying to find out something? Anything? He wasn't going to tell us anything unless he didn't see us as a threat," I said, feeling like I needed to explain.

"You are absolutely correct," Logan said through his laughter. "I'm just wondering why I never thought to bring you along before."

"You didn't realize the superpower of a middle aged mom," I said primly.

He laughed harder.

I sat back, waiting for him to get hold of himself.

Logan wiped at his eyes, and then looked over at me, the smile lingering around the corners of his mouth. "You did great, and I appreciate it. He may not have suspected you, although he wasn't sure if you were putting on a show, but he suspected me of everything." His smile dropped as he leaned back against the seat of the car.

"Okay, what about the other guy?" I asked.

"The one we saw right before we left?"

I nodded.

"I don't know, but he smelled like dark magic."

"Like the necromancer that was after me?"

Logan shook his head. "No, it's different. I mean, they're all bad, and doing things they shouldn't, but this wasn't the same group of magical stink."

"Does bad magic stink?" I asked, thinking about my earlier musing on the idea.

"It does to me. Remember, I'm more sensitive to smell." He tapped his nose.

"You are. I didn't smell a thing. But he was glaring to beat the band," I said.

"He knows something about why we were there," Logan said with a surety I didn't feel. "I've filed his face and smell away should he show up later in all this."

"I wish I could disagree and just call you paranoid, but I can't." I thought about the man, and then Rochester. "I'm astounded Rochester didn't look at you and see Evander."

Logan shrugged. "People see what they want to. I don't look anything like the sophisticated Evander Thane."

"Will you start using that name again?" I asked.

"What?" His head jerked toward me.

"Will you use the name Evander Thane again?"

"Why would I?"

"Because it's your name," I said.

"It was," Logan said. "But I see all this information about Evander, about me," he corrected himself, "And

I don't feel a thing. He's like a complete stranger to me."

"Well, not really," I said.

"What do you mean?"

"I didn't talk with you as Evander all that much, but even though you lost your memory, you didn't lose that part of you that makes you you," I said. "You have the same level of confidence, of awareness of your strengths. And you're not afraid of danger," I added, thinking about the brief conversation I'd had with Evander-Logan about the danger he faced.

"That's good to hear," Logan said finally. "I didn't think about it like that. I'm not feeling all that jazzed about my former self."

"I can't help you with that," I said. "But I saw more in common than differences. You're the same man."

"Gods, I hope not," Logan said. "I did some pretty questionable things as Evander from what I've found. The things I've been able to find make me wonder what isn't on the record."

"Well, then maybe you lose that part of who you used to be. Although I seem to recall that we had a conversation about stealing and your current career," I said.

"Fine, fine," Logan said, rolling his eyes.

Laughing, I allowed him to change the subject. He'd gotten the use of a friend's apartment close to the police station, and we talked about where we would go to dinner.

While at dinner, I noted that Logan Gentry did, in fact, have a lot of what I'd seen in Evander Thane. He was smooth, and easy to speak with, and conversational on many subjects. He asked me a lot about living on Martha's Vineyard, harking back to our conversation earlier in the day.

Toward the end of dinner, I asked, "So what do you think about meeting with the detective today? And that man at the end?" I didn't know if I wanted to talk about it, but I kept worrying about it in my mind—so I brought it up.

"You realize that I've survived since Mark found me in the desert because I indulge at times in my deep paranoia?" Logan asked without skipping a beat.

"No, I didn't, but it makes sense."

"Well, when he was showing us the photos, and listing the names, all I could think was, Why did these people want Evander out of the way? And the guy you knew —Tomas—you said he wasn't a major player, from what you could tell. Someone more on the outside than on the inside. That tells me there was something behind me ending up dumped in a desert. That there's something at play here we're not seeing." His face hardened.

"My thoughts as well. What are you going to do?"

"I can't do much until I get access to Evander's accounts, and his files. Believe it or not," Logan looked at me, "the files are tougher than the money."

"I believe it," I said. "Can I do anything to help?"

Logan shook his head. "You've done enough. You've probably put yourself out more than you should have, if I'm being honest. But I'm a on a quest, so I'll set aside my guilt."

I didn't smile. His comment was too close to what Florry had been saying.

"We also need to talk about what service you would like from me," Logan continued.

"I don't know," I said. "I've been thinking about it, and I haven't come up with anything."

"When you do, let me know. Without you, I couldn't have found my past."

"I don't know about that," I said.

"I do. I don't move in the same circles as Evander, and my job is such that I do my best to stay in the shadows."

"Yes, but that guy, that last client, the one who knew you as someone else—you really think he is going to keep his mouth shut? I hate to say it, but he seemed pretty untrustworthy."

"He is," Logan said. "I would like to go and just threaten him a bit more, but I promised Peter I wouldn't contact him again."

"He didn't know your real name anyway," I said. "Caleb Montgomery, remember?"

Logan nodded. "That's true. He's the kind of guy who would have been happy to have something on Evander Thane, so I think it's okay to think he didn't know Caleb and Evander were the same. I'm not assuming, mind you. He's also the kind of guy who would sit on this kind of information until it worked in his best interest."

"He's a weasel, that's for sure. Lots of them showing up lately," I said, thinking not only of Peter Dunleavy, but of Scott Trenton, the Oak Bluffs police officer who suspected me of everything he could think of.

Logan didn't say anything. What could he say? I figured that I'd be seeing more weasels the more I got into this.

After dinner, Logan directed the driver to the place he'd secured for us to stay the night. It was nice, obviously professionally decorated, and the room I was in had its own bathroom, which I was glad to see. I got into my pajamas, and went out to the galley kitchen to see if there was some tea, or something hot to drink.

Logan was in the small living room on the sofa, the news on the television with the sound down, drinking a beer.

My phone rang where I'd left it on the table behind the sofa. In checking it, it came up Restricted. I'd just had one of these—when was it? Oh, that's right, when I went to the apothecary to place my order for the bulk herbs.

"You going to answer that?" Logan asked without turning around.

"No. It's not coming up on caller ID. I don't answer those."

He made a noncommittal noise.

I went back to searching for tea. Finally, I found a chamomile blend in the back of one of the cupboards, and filled the kettle.

My phone made the noise that indicated there was a voicemail. I sighed. I'd need to listen to it, just to make sure it wasn't something I needed to know. That was how people got you, even on your cell phone. You worried about missing some piece of important information.

"Hi. My name is Inspector Farrah Lockwood, with the New England division of the Magical Law Enforcement Department. If our information is correct, you have assumed a new mantle of responsibility. If that is the case and I'm speaking to the right person, please call me at 848-555-2727. I gave you a call earlier. I'd appreciate hearing back from you. Thank you." The voicemail ended.

I listened to it again. This woman, whoever she was, spoke very carefully on the message. I noticed she didn't use my name, or mention what responsibility I'd taken on. I appreciated it. Although I wondered if she couldn't say—didn't know, maybe? There were so many rules around being the Oracle and who could access her that I didn't understand. Things like this message made me wonder if it was all a sham, and I wasn't safe at all.

The kettle whistled, making me jump. I made my tea, my thoughts troubled.

"You okay?" Logan came up behind me.

"I don't know," I said. "I think…" I stopped, wondering how much to tell him.

"What?"

"I wish I understood more about how the Oracle is safe, how we stay safe," I said.

"What happened?" His eyes were sharp and bright, focused on me.

"I got a call from the magical police."

"Why?"

I shook my head. "She was very vague, but she seems to know that I'm the Oracle. How can they know? I thought you had to do the fire ceremony, and prove yourself worthy of meeting with the Oracle!" Saying the words out loud made the ball of panic in my chest explode outward, unfettered, throughout me.

"Hey, hang on. Why don't you ask the guide? Your mentor? And see?"

"That's what I need to do. I'm going to my room," I said. "I'm sorry, but I am not going to be good company for anyone."

"No worries here," Logan said, his eyes softer than before. "Let me know if you need anything."

I walked to my room, tea in hand. I liked that he didn't try to solve anything for me. Not that he could—this was my problem. But I liked that he left me to handle it. Derek would have—I stopped myself. It didn't matter what Derek would have done. He wasn't here anymore. And I was still mad at him. I hated being mad at him, but I had no idea when the anger would dissipate.

Shutting the door, I pulled the grimoire out of my bag. I didn't feel good about leaving it even without Florry's warnings. So while it weighed a ton, for me, it was right to have it close by.

"Florry, Goldie, somebody. I could use some help," I said. I added Goldie as a second thought. He'd been pretty quiet for the last day or so since the bull barged into my house again.

"What's up?" Florry materialized, a cigarette in her mouth. Today, she was garbed in a bright yellow scarf that was tied in her hair, a pink nightgown, and a canary yellow housedress over the nightie. The slippers weren't her usual fluffy numbers, but a white terry cloth pair with pink roses all over them.

"Very festive," I said, nodding at her.

"My summer duds," Florry said. "We're not here to talk about how comfortable I am in death. What's going on?"

Instead of answering, I played the voicemail.

There was silence after it ended.

"How am I supposed to be safe when just anyone can find me?" I said. The tears that were threatening to fall made my throat hurt.

"Okay, first, no one can just find you. The magical po po have to do the fire ceremony just like everyone else. Unlike everyone else, they can use the coordinates to figure out who you are, and what your contact information is. So calm down." Florry took a drag on her cigarette.

"Second, you have to talk to them. That's part of the gig. I mean, in all honesty, you don't owe them diddly, and if they get too pushy, which they've been known to do, you can tell them to pound sand and to get the heck out of your home."

"I don't want to deal with the police. I have enough of that in my non-Oracle life." I was still a suspect with my local police in the disappearance of Ashton Flint, the presumed former owner of Goldie.

"Well, they're gonna try to get you to work with them, tell you that it's your duty, you'll be helping the greater good, blah blah blah. Tell them to get stuffed. That's not your gig, or your responsibility. They'll hope that you don't know better." She rolled her eyes. "They never learn."

"You're not making me feel better."

Florry shrugged, her hands spread wide. "Hey, I don't manage the cops. It's just part of doing business in these modern times. You just need to set your boundaries, and I'm gonna tell you, you're not being too harsh. You're never too harsh. They'll use you if they can, so you do what you need to for you."

"I don't have to work for them?"

"Nope. We don't answer to anyone. The Oracle is her own person. No one directs her. Which of course, drives our magical po po *ba-na-nas*," she said, drawing out the last word.

I had to laugh. I could see, in that one word, how Florry had been a pain in the backside for any officer who had to deal with her.

"Don't sweat it, Wynter. You have plenty to worry about, but this isn't it. Now that they've found you, expect a visit."

"Okay. Thank you," I said. "It's nice that you come to help when I need it."

"Don't get used to it. I have things to do," Florry grumped at me. "Where's Goldie?"

"He hasn't been around since Ariadne and the bull showed up again."

Florry rolled her eyes. "That nutter. I wish the gods or whatever they are would rein her in."

"There are gods?" I asked.

"Sure. Myths have to come from somewhere. There's a lot more truth in the myths than humans know. Or want to know," she added.

"Thank you for coming," I said. "I really needed to talk to you. It would be nice if you showed up more often, like when I need help."

"I'm not a dog, toots. And I keep telling you this, even though you're not listening, but each Oracle has to find her way."

I sighed. "Thanks, I guess."

You're doing well, Goldie spoke then.

"That would be nice to hear a bit more often," I said, unable to stop my response.

Florry is right. You have to do most of this on your own. How else will you learn?

"Is this still a test?" I asked, struck by a sudden thought.

"Maybe," Florry said. "I think it's more a reality check, myself. This isn't an easy gig. You might as well get used to it, to the way things are."

"Why do people want this?" I asked, falling back into the pillows.

"It's a great honor. It's a lot of power. You hold a lot of cards. You just don't see it yet. You have to stop being afraid," Florry said with no hesitation.

"What?"

"I said what I said, sugar. Now, anything else? Am I all caught up on current events?"

"No, I think I'm good. Relatively speaking. And you know what I do," I said.

"All right. I'm off. Later, Goldie." Her voice was fond.

Tell her goodnight, Goldie said.

"He says goodnight," I said.

"Thanks," Florry smiled. Then she was gone.

"I think it's sweet that you two miss each other," I said.

Goldie didn't respond.

"Hey, I have a question. I've been meaning to ask you. Do I have to talk out loud to talk with you?" I asked.

No. I can hear your thoughts if you direct them to me.

Taking a breath, I thought, *So, Goldie, you can't just listen in to whatever I'm thinking about?*

No, thank the gods. I don't want to be privy to all your thoughts. But we can communicate without you having to speak.

That would be good, I thought. *I was thinking about this when the bull showed up the other night.*

It's good for exactly that kind of situation, Goldie replied. *Florry is right, Wynter. Meet with the officers and then send them on their way. You hold all the power in this meeting.*

It doesn't feel like it, I thought.

In this, Florry is right once more. Your fear is keeping you from seeing the truth.

I am afraid, I thought.

I can feel it, he replied. *You should not be. There is more protecting you than you think.*

"I guess I have to take your word for it," I said out loud.

You do.

"Thanks," I said. I got up and brushed my teeth, and then crawled into bed, turning off the light on the nightstand.

I didn't dream, and when I woke to a room full of sunshine, I felt good. The ferry ride back to the Vineyard, while long, was uneventful. Logan and I took turns napping. Once we were back on Martha's Vineyard, Logan drove us back to my house.

"I'm going to be traveling for the rest of the week," he said. "And I'm going to see if I can find a place to rent."

"I didn't tell you about the rentals around here to kick you out," I said. I felt bad, like he might feel pressured to leave.

"No, I didn't think you did," Logan replied. "But if I have to do more traveling, I'm going to ask my friend Mark to come and stay, to be here if you need help. I feel like I owe this to you for continuing to help me. This isn't the agreed upon service, either," he added. "I just would feel better. We still don't know who the necromancer who attacked you was, or who he and the man in the blue van works for, and I..." he stopped, shrugging. "I'll feel better."

I really wished that I could just forget about the man who had accosted me in the grocery store and then my house would become a thing of the past, but that didn't seem to be something that would happen any time soon.

There had also been a van following me and parked outside my house. Logan had scared the man inside the van off—but he said that he could tell the necromancer guy had been in the van. That the man in the van and my attacker were connected. Who both of these men were working for, what they wanted outside of Goldie—just one more set of things I didn't know. It was extremely frustrating.

"All right," I said. "As long as we're clear I'm not trying to be an ungracious hostess."

"No one could ever accuse you of that, Wynter," Logan said. The sharp planes of his face softened as he looked at me. His eyes glinted gold.

I couldn't look away. I could feel every inch of my skin vibrate under his gaze.

Logan broke our contact first. "I'll be in my room for the rest of the night. No need to cook for me. I'll be going out later." He gave me a nod.

It took me a minute to figure out that he meant his panther would be going out later. Which meant his panther would be eating. Oh, good night, Maggie. "Here? On the island? Aren't you worried people might see you?"

"They'll just think I'm one of the crazy things that washes ashore," he said. His grin had a slightly more feral look than normal. His excitement shone from his eyes.

"No pets!" I shouted at his disappearing back.

His laughter echoed down the stairs.

CHAPTER SIX

*a*fter his nighttime prowl, Logan left the house early the next morning. He'd been gone for two days. In that time, Shelly, my best friend, had come over for dinner and we'd sat until late last night talking about not only being the Oracle, but what was next in terms of the other Mrs. Chastain.

"I think I'll invite them out here," I said.

"You sure you want to do that?" Shelly asked.

We were out back, stretched out in the lawn chairs, looking up at the night sky. The sea was especially fragrant this evening. I could smell the salt air, and knew that if I was out here for another hour, my clothing would be damp with salt.

But I didn't mind. It was the smell of my home.

Which made me think of Tethys, and her most recent message. I wondered what the sea would reveal, what kind of choice would be required from me. I hadn't told anyone about the second message. It felt… private. Like something that was mine, for me. She'd called me daughter, something she hadn't done the first time she made contact.

"I think so," I said, returning to the conversation with Shelly. "Maybe not right away. But I know that Maud and Donovan were planning to invite them to stay. So maybe I'll piggyback onto that." I stretched, feeling at ease for the first time in what felt like forever. "I'll ask Rachel to inquire."

"That might be better. A more structured schedule, less time you have to be together, in case things go poorly," Shelly agreed. "I feel like you need to take this one slow."

"I'd like to take everything slow," I said. "That doesn't seem to be a choice I necessarily get."

Even with my whining, it was good to spend time with her. I got up the next morning feeling refreshed, and ready for anything.

Hopefully, I'd be meeting a second consultant soon. Now that I'd helped Logan, it felt like it was time. But Florry had said they came at random intervals, determined more by the potential consultants and those who proved themselves worthy than anything I did.

So, while it was difficult, I waited.

The day was so beautiful, I decided that I'd go for a walk on the beach. I'd taken our dogs when the kids were younger, but after Moose, our last dog, had passed away, I didn't get another dog. The kids were in college, and I just hated having to lose my furry family members.

The beach was already beginning to fill up with families. I turned north and headed to a part of the beach where it wasn't so crowded. There were more rocks along the shoreline, and the water was rougher.

Breathing in, I turned my face upward to the sun. It was gorgeous, and the smell of the sea made me feel happy.

A different scent hit my nose, right in the middle of my mini-sun worship, sharp and strong and stinky. I blinked and looked around. Ravens were overhead, circling lazily, focused on a point below them, a point just off the beach.

There was a lump about twenty feet from me, in the water, bumping against the rocks.

For a moment, I just stared. I knew what it was, without having to get any closer, without having to do anything—but my brain didn't want to register what it was I was seeing.

I don't know how long I stood, staring. Then I looked down the beach—I needed to make sure that none of the kids down there saw this. It would scar them for life. I was a lot older, and the image of that still, lumpy figure was seared into my brain.

God, I didn't want to, but I had to go and look. I didn't want to call the cops and get busted for making a phony phone call.

Carefully, I picked my way across the rocks until I stood right next to the lump. I shooed away a raven that had landed on a rock on the other side of the lump—the person. It squawked as it rose into the air to join the rest of the ravens still circling.

Up close, I could see the back of the person's head. The wet hair could be blond, but it was too dark for me to tell, given how wet they were. I squatted down, and gingerly tugged at the dark shirt, trying to turn the body a bit without touching him or her.

As the face came into view, I fell backward, landing painfully on my right hip. Once I stopped falling, I sat and stared.

It was the blond necromancer.

The last time I'd seen him, he'd been coming for me in my living room, a snarl on his face and nothing but bad intentions on his mind. I'd sent him somewhere and hadn't seen him since—what was it? Four, maybe five weeks? Something like that. My mind couldn't think straight.

How had he gotten here?

More importantly, had I killed him?

I felt panic race through me, making me sweat, and unable to move. What did I do now? I was the last person, presumably, to see this man alive. The fact that he had been intending to hurt me — *Kill you*, Goldie said quietly.

"What?" I whispered.

He was going to kill you to get to me. It would not have worked, but that wasn't going to stop him. Had you not sent him on his way, you would have died, Wynter. His tone brooked no discussion.

"I'm sorry," I gasped. I wanted him gone, not dead gone. His face was pale with a gray undertone, and it was clear that he'd been in the water for a while. The things that lived in the sea had been taking bites of his pale face, leaving him patched and grotesque looking. It wasn't pretty.

This is what can happen when you set out to harm others, Goldie said.

"He's dead," I whispered. When I'd thought about this earlier, I hadn't felt any guilt about what might happen to this man. Not after he'd come after me.

Now? The guilt was nearly overwhelming. Had I killed him? *Goldie, did I kill him?*

Goldie didn't reply.

Somehow, I managed to stand up, and make my way back to the beach. My instinct was to turn and run back to my house. Lock the door, close the blinds, and hide. Hope that someone else found him, called it in.

But I couldn't do that.

I'd taken on a responsibility to help people who came to me. This guy wasn't a consultant, and Goldie was right. He'd been planning to hurt me. But now, he couldn't hurt me. He'd never hurt anyone again. I didn't know if that was because of me, or just a side effect of me sending him somewhere.

I sighed. My hands fumbled as I searched for my phone in my pocket. Once I got hold of the phone, I pulled it out and promptly dropped it.

"Pull it together, Chastain," I said, trying to infuse some courage into myself. I picked up the phone and slowly and carefully dialed 911.

"911, what's your emergency?" a woman's voice asked.

"I'm at the Oak Bluffs beach," I said, my voice sounding high and anxious to my ears. "On the southern end, near the rocks. There's a body trapped in the rocks."

"A body?" The woman's voice stayed calm. "Have you gone over to look at it?"

"Yes," I said. "It's a person."

"Okay, Miss—"

"Chastain. Wynter Chastain," I said.

"Okay, Wynter, I want you to stay right there, and we'll have officers there shortly," the woman said. "Are you all right?"

"I guess," I said.

"Would you like me to stay on the phone with you?" the woman asked.

"How long before the officers get here?" I replied.

"They are two minutes out," she said.

"Then no, thank you. I'll just wait here until they get here."

"Okay. Please call back if anything changes, Wynter," she said.

I ended the call, hugging my arms around myself. The sun didn't feel as bright anymore.

Within a short amount of time, I heard a siren, and a police car with the lights on pulled to a stop at the end of the parking lot closest to where I stood. Two officers headed toward me. I raised a hand, waving to them.

As they got closer, my hand and my heart dropped.

Andy Dentwhistle and Scott Trenton. For Pete's sake—were there any other officers in the local police department?

I steeled my face into what I hoped was a neutral upset look.

"Wynter," Andy said as he came down the bluff, sliding a bit at the bottom on the sand. "What have you found?"

I pointed. "He's right over there."

"You look at it?" Scott Trenton squinted out at the lump.

"Yes. Just like I told the 911 operator," I said, not in the mood for Scott Trenton.

"You know him?" Scott asked, not bothering to hide his sneer.

"No. I have no idea who he is," I said. Which was the truth.

Andy walked out on the rocks, bending down to peer at the necromancer. "Yep," he called back, "It's a body."

I resisted the urge to roll my eyes.

Andy walked back with a lot more grace than I had, coming to a stop next to Scott. "Let's get the medical examiner out here."

Scott nodded and walked off, his phone to his ear.

"What can you tell me?" Andy asked.

I shook my head, wrapping my arms around myself again. "Nothing, really. I was out for a walk today, and I saw it. I walked over to see if it was a body. I didn't want any of the kids on the beach to find it," I added. "I thought it was a person, but to see it…" my voice trailed off.

Andy nodded. "It's a shock, if you've never seen anyone who has died before." His voice held an unspoken question.

"I never have," I said, even though it irritated me that he'd ask. He knew me. He'd known me his entire life. He knew I'd never seen a dead body.

Scott came back. "They're on their way. Wynter, do you know this man?"

I shook my head. "As I told you, I have no idea who he is." I closed my eyes, not wanting to see that blank face, but unable to shake the vision of it.

"This is becoming a habit for you. Missing people, and now someone is dead," Scott said.

You know how you can be doing something, and your mind is pulled in a couple of different directions, and afterwards, you are astounded you got anything done? That's where I was. At Scott's words, and more importantly, what he didn't say, my entire focus snapped and my mind felt crystal clear. I took a breath and met his eyes. "What are you insinuating, Officer Trenton?"

"Now, Wynter—" Andy began.

"No, I'd like to hear what she has to say," Scott said with a nasty emphasis on the word 'she'.

"Well, here is what *she* has to say," I put my hands on my hips and took a step toward Scott Denton. "I have no idea who this man is. I wish that I did. I wish that I could help you. I can't. I've done the right thing. I called the police, so this man wouldn't be left out here, so that no child would find him. As to this becoming a habit, I have done nothing wrong, Officer Trenton. If you believe I have, then you need to make that clear, and file a report to move things forward."

I stopped to take a breath. "If not," I narrowed my eyes, feeling a swell of power pulling me up straight, to the point where I felt ten feet tall, "You need to immediately cease casting aspersion on me and my character. You're not from here, but I am. And I can tell you, that when you cast stones without reason, people don't forget. I certainly won't." I took a breath, the air filling my lungs. I didn't look away from Scott Trenton.

What was this, this surge of power, of confidence, and of surety? I didn't know, but I liked it.

He gazed at me for a moment, and then his eyes slid away.

That's what I thought. He was a weasel, and a coward.

Above, the ravens scattered with a raucous set of calls. They flew inland. I wondered where they were going. Inland was calm after a dead body sighting.

"Let's all bring it down," Andy said.

"I am fine, Andy," I said. I was. The shakiness and nerves from just ten minutes ago were gone. I was the Oracle, and I wasn't going to be bullied by this small little man. I sent the necromancer away from me, but I didn't kill him. At least, I hoped not. Regardless, I wasn't going to let this little mean man bully me any further.

Whatever either officer was about to say was interrupted by the medical examiner and two of her assistants coming down the bluff with a stretcher. The woman in front was tall for a woman, with orange hair pulled into a haphazard bun. As she got closer, I could see that she had freckles across her cheeks and nose. She gave a brief smile.

"Andy, Scott," she said, nodding. She looked at me. "I'm Dr. Mamie Marshall." She stuck out a hand.

"Wynter Chastain."

"Who found the deceased?" Dr. Marshall asked. She had a slight accent, but I couldn't place it.

"I did," I said.

Dr. Marshall peppered me with questions as she pulled on gloves, and then with another curt nod, walked out to where the necromancer still floated.

"Is it possible for me to go home?" I asked.

"You can go—" Scott began.

"Yes," Andy cut his partner off with a glare. "We may need to come by if there are any other questions, but go on home, Wynter."

"Okay," I said. "I have no plans to travel, and you know where I live," I said. Then I turned and walked home without looking back once. I'd seen enough.

As I left the beach and walked toward my house, a thought hit me. Tethys had said that the sea eventually revealed everything, and that I'd have to make a choice. Well, it had certainly revealed a lot.

I wasn't sure I liked it. I had, however, made a choice.

I could have walked away, but that wasn't who I was, and in my opinion, that wasn't the way that someone who had a responsibility to help others behaved. I'd made my choice. I was the Oracle, and I would act accordingly. Not only would I take on my responsibility, but I would not allow myself to be pushed around. Not anymore.

I could still feel the surge of power running through me. It was like little electric shocks that came out at the end of my fingertips. Was this part of being the Oracle? Or having magic? I'd have to ask Florry. Whatever it was, I liked it. I'd been pretty mild mannered most of my life, taking care of others, and always putting myself last. How could I not? I was married, with three children all close in age. That's what you did.

But now?

I was responsible for myself. And while I would help people as the Oracle, I'd put myself first every now and again as well. I had to think that telling Scott Jerk Trenton to back off was high on the list of self-care.

My feet made their way home without me even thinking about it. Which was good. I was caught up in what this new thing meant. When I walked up the steps to my porch, my step was light, and while I felt bad that Stinky had somehow ended up in the water, there was no guarantee that's where I sent him. He seemed like the kind of guy who had a lot of people who didn't like him.

"Wynter Chastain?" a woman's voice said.

My scream echoed around the porch.

CHAPTER SEVEN

"Who are you?" I scream-whispered once I'd found my voice, backing myself toward the railing of the porch.

The woman, petite and dark-haired, took a step back, her hands up. "Hey, I'm sorry, I didn't mean to scare you. I thought you saw me. I'm Farrah Lockwood, and I'm with the Magical Law Enforcement department. I called you the other day?"

I stopped. "You did. I didn't call you back," I said pointedly.

"No, but we've—I've—trying to get in touch with you. We've taken turns doing the fire ceremony, and it finally worked for me. I wouldn't be here if my intentions weren't good." Her hands were still up, and she hadn't come any closer to me since I'd screamed.

"That's true," I said finally. "Okay. You can come in." I knew what this meant, even if Detective Farrah didn't.

She was my next consultant.

I wondered how that worked with her job. I wondered if anyone at her work had told her what it meant. Well, I'd soon find out.

Farrah followed me inside, and when I stopped to set down my keys on the small hall table, I saw her looking around.

"This is a great house," she said. "All the houses here are so cute."

"We used to be a summer camp colony," I said.

"It shows. I love them. Do you live here year round?"

I wasn't sure I liked that question, but she wouldn't be here if she had bad intentions toward me. "I do. I have my entire life."

"What a great place," Farrah sighed. "I loved the ferry ride over."

"I love living here," I said. "Now come in and let's talk, Officer Lockwood."

"Oh, please call me Farrah," she said.

In the light of the kitchen, Farrah Lockwood was petite, as I'd initially thought. She had dark hair that was pulled into a neat braid down her back, with golden skin. Her eyes were light—gray, I realized with a shock. They gave her a piercing look, even now, as she smiled.

"Would you like some tea?" I asked.

"Yes, please. That would be perfect," Farrah said.

Neither of us spoke as I filled the kettle and switched it on. I pulled down two cups, taking my time to fuss with the tea things. "What does magical law enforcement want with me?" I asked, without turning around.

"Well, first we need to determine that you're the newest Oracle of Theama," Farrah said.

I turned then. "What do you think I am, if not the Oracle?"

She laughed, her laughter easy. "Hey, I'm just doing the work. I don't make the rules."

"I am the Oracle of Theama," I said.

"You've accepted it?" Farrah asked. "Formally?"

"I have," I said. How did she—they—know about that? That was interesting.

There is a lot of information about the Oracle, about most seers, that is passed around, Goldie chimed in then. *Don't worry.*

"Okay, one question down. There's really only one other question, then," Farrah said.

I leaned against the counter. "What's that?"

"Will you help us?" Her face was open, her eyes wide.

She was good, I thought. "No," I said.

"Why?"

"The Oracle doesn't work that way. I think you, or at least, your bosses, know that," I smiled, so I didn't sound so harsh. "I will, however, help you with something, Detective Farrah Lockwood."

"What's that?" she asked.

"Let me help you find the answer you're looking for." I stared at her, trying to get a sense what a woman who presented as competent and together could be seeking. "What is it that you need answered, that no one else has been able to answer?" I never spoke like this, but as I did, I knew it was the right thing to say.

Farrah's eyes widened a fraction. "Why would you ask that?"

"You couldn't have found me if you didn't need my help," I said with a shrug as the kettle clicked off. "What do you seek?" I busied myself with pouring the water into the teapot, giving Farrah time to answer.

"My mother." The words fell flat, with the weight of the world behind them.

I turned to see a young woman with eyes older than they should be. Farrah was older than my children, but not by much.

"What happened?" I asked. I put a cup in front of her.

Farrah's hands wrapped around the cup, although I'd bet my hat she didn't know what she was doing.

"She had an overnight shift. She was a nurse, an ICU nurse. She called to let Dad know she was on her way home, and she… she never came home." The last word disappeared almost as though it had never been spoken.

"Would she have left?" I asked. It was a hurtful thing, and I knew it, but I had to ask.

Farrah was shaking her head before I finished asking. "No. She loved her life. She and Dad—they had a hard time when they first got together. He met her when he was in Egypt, when he was working with Doctors without Borders. She was a nursing student, helping the doctors out in their clinic. They fell in love. Her family wasn't happy, her marrying an American. They're good now," she waved a hand.

I heard the struggle in her words though, how hard it had been for her parents.

"She and Dad were in love until the day she disappeared. It was almost embarrassing, how much they loved each other. She called, like she always did when she had a late shift, and then… nothing." Farrah looked down at the cup in her hands. "She never came back."

"I'm sorry," I said. "I can't imagine how that must feel."

"It's awful," she said, her voice low. "It's the wondering. You never stop wondering. Is she gone? Is she hurt? Is she okay? Did she leave because she wanted to?" Farrah looked up then, and the pain was stark in her eyes.

"How long ago was this?" I asked.

"I was fourteen," Farrah said.

She didn't have to say more. As she spoke, I knew that I was supposed to help her find out the truth about her mother. "I can help you," I said carefully. I wanted to be clear. "But I can't promise an outcome. How many people used the fire ceremony before you tried?" I asked.

Farrah blinked, clearly not thinking about work at all. "Um… six, maybe seven?"

"None of you thought it was odd that you were the one who was successful?"

A hint of pink flashed across the top of her cheeks. "There was comment that it was maybe due to the fact that we're both women," she said.

I could tell the suggestion had made her angry. "Nonsense. My first consultant was not a woman."

"Is he still here?" Farrah's eyes brightened.

That was odd. Why would she care about another consultant? "No," I said. I may not know all the rules but I wasn't discussing one consultant with another. "Now, tell me about your mother. Was she active with any volunteering? Politics? Did she advocate for things that might make people angry?"

"You don't think I looked into that when I became a cop?" Farrah asked. "Mom was the one who had magic. And Dad didn't know. She told me when I was eight, that her family had always had some extra talents, extra skills. We couldn't talk about it around anyone else, not even my Dad."

Farrah's eyes grew distant, and whatever she was seeing, I'd bet it wasn't me.

"It was really hard, trying to keep the secret from my dad. Mom was close to tears when she told me. She said it was the only secret she'd ever kept from him, but she was obligated to, bound by blood and tradition. That's what she said, blood and tradition."

"What kind of tradition?" I asked. I wasn't sure where to go with this.

"We were doing magic. Like making small spells, herbs and chanting, that kind of thing. I was learning how to use them. She said that once I reached womanhood, there would be so much more. I was fourteen, so I asked, when does that happen? I'm not a little kid anymore. Mom rolled her eyes and said I'd know."

"When you got your period?" I asked.

"I guess. I noticed that I could hear things, like the thoughts of people, not really full thoughts, but like when you hear someone talking around a corner. And I know it's weird, but it's almost like I could hear animals, although I haven't been able to hear them in a long time. After Mom disappeared, her family, especially Nonna, my grandmother, and my aunt Panya, came to see me regularly. They looked at me, like they were expecting something." Farrah shook her head.

I could see the years of disappointment on her. "What were they looking for?"

"I have no idea," Farrah said. "They would never tell me. They still come to visit, although not as much, and they don't give me the searching looking anymore."

That suggested that they were looking for something that Farrah had, something their family had? They expected her to have it, and when she didn't—what had gone wrong? What was Farrah supposed to have? A thing? A gift?

Interesting.

"Well, I think I can work with that," I said, although honestly, I was wondering how to go about this. "Do you have somewhere to stay?"

"I do," Farrah said. Her professional self took over. "And I do need to talk with you about working with us."

"No can do," Florry said, appearing off to the side of the island where Farrah sat. "They know this, and yet here she is."

I held up my hand.

"What?" Farrah said.

"You're not the only person here," I replied, enjoying the shock that showed itself in her raised eyebrows. "The Oracle doesn't work like that, and your superiors know this. While I may be new to my role, I'm not unaware. There's a reason that none of the six or seven people who tried to find me before you did could. They were not seeking something that was worthy. Your office wants me to do your work for you. That's not going to happen." It felt weird to be so firm, but after what Florry had said about the Magical Law Enforcement department earlier, I was irritated. Why bother me?

At least their efforts brought me a new consultant. Logan might be put out, I thought as I stifled a very unprofessional giggle. He'd gotten used to having my full attention.

"What's cat boy gonna do now?" Florry asked, as though reading my mind.

I couldn't see her but she sounded amused. She would be.

"Shush," I said to her. "Not you," I said to Farrah.

"Who are you talking to?" Farrah's eyes were bright as she tried to discreetly look around the room.

"Those who speak to me," I said, and tried to keep a straight face. It sounded so formal, almost pompous, but little gems like this kept falling out of my mouth without me even realizing it.

"You tell her," Florry said.

"I want you to stick around," I said to Florry, turning my head. I still couldn't see her. "We need to speak." Then I turned back to Farrah. "Will you write down your mother's basic information for me? Where you lived, where she worked, what she looked like, her age and full name? That kind of thing?" I pulled a notepad and a pen from the junk drawer in the island. "That will help me." Sliding it over to Farrah, I turned, and went out onto the porch.

"You're in a twist," Florry commented, finally drifting into my line of vision.

"You're darn right," I said, pushing aside Farrah Lockwood and her concerns for a moment. "Did you happen to be out and about earlier today? Did you see what I found?"

"No, what?" Florry was unconcerned.

"The necromancer!" I hissed. "The blond man, the one who—you know, was here," I jerked my head toward where Farrah sat in the kitchen, not wanting to say more.

"Oh, the one who tried to knock you over the head and steal Goldie?"

"Yes, that one," I whispered. "He is on the beach, deader than a doornail, as we speak."

"Well, he was trying to kill you," Florry looked unconcerned.

"Did I do that? Send him to his death? Drop him in the middle of the ocean?" My words were barely above a whisper, but Florry heard me.

"I don't know. You certainly whooshed him out of your house. This would indicate that you do, in fact, need to practice the whole whooshing thing. Y'know, like we talked about."

Her words brought back the conversation with Tethys. *You are strong if you choose to be.* That's what she'd said. An odd combination of words. *If you choose to be.* Was this the choice she referred to? I felt like I'd made a choice when I called the police after finding the blond man's body. But maybe there was more to this.

Of course, there was more to this. There was always more. I sighed.

"What?" Florry asked.

"Tethys came to me again. When I was on the ferry on the way to New York."

Florry shook her head, and a cigarette appeared in her hand.

I was so thankful I didn't have to smell them.

"I don't know what it is about you, Wynter. The bull lady. One of the ancient guardians of the sea. I'm not sure if I should be pea green with envy, because this suggests you have big doings headed your way, or offer you my sympathy."

"That's surprising, coming from you," I said.

"Just trying to look at the situation objectively. I have a suggestion for you regarding cat boy. About the service he's promised you."

"I'm listening."

"The next time someone needs to be dealt with, you hand it off to him."

I stared at her. "Isn't that kind of a waste? I mean, hurting—"

"Or killing," Florry interjected.

"Doesn't seem like something I should ask for."

"You're worried about protection, right? Make him protect you when it's necessary."

I shook my head. "That doesn't feel right."

She sighed. "It was a suggestion. How do you plan to settle your nerves, then? You need to get yourself together."

"You don't think I'm together?" I asked, feeling stung by her words.

"I think you're nervous, and it makes you question yourself."

"Well, maybe if you offered me a little more help, some more guidance. You and Goldie are pretty darn tight lipped, always telling me each Oracle has to find her own way!" My voice rose with my anger, and I did my best to throttle it back down. "I'm trying to find my own way, and frankly, I don't want to die. There have been a lot of people around who want me to die. So maybe take that into consideration when you're judging me."

Florry stared at me, blinking once, and then smiled. "There you are. There's the Oracle."

"Shut up," I looked away.

"You've let your family and those around you drive your life for a long time, my girl," Florry said. "Now you're in the driver's seat. It's time to get comfy. That's where you're going to be for the foreseeable future. People always try to boot you out of it, even more so now that you've got power they don't. I need you to plant your butt and not move for anyone."

"This is some kind of tough love lesson?" I asked incredulously.

"Yes. You need it." Florry was cheerful.

In fact, she didn't sound sorry at all.

"And you need to get rid of the magical Po Po girl, and do some practicing with your flower pots. Yeah, yeah, I know she's the consultant, but you can scry later and see what's what." She waved her hand. "Your consultants, you'll learn, aren't going anywhere. They're like barnacles. Once they show up, you'll have to escort them out. Look at cat boy," Florry added with a wicked grin. "You can't pry him loose."

"Shut up," I said again.

"But you need to practice the thing that is for you, Wynter, your magic that will keep you safe." There was no humor as Florry spoke, leaning in. "That's the most important thing."

"You're sure?" I asked.

"I might not be giving you what you think you need, but I'm giving you what I know you need. Yes. I'm sure."

I stared at her, waiting to see if there was anything more forthcoming.

Instead, she leaned back, one arm across her chest and tucked under the opposite elbow as she exhaled smoke from the ever-present cigarette. "Goddess, I love that I can smoke these now without a care in the world." She looked out at the street and then back at me. "What are you waiting for?"

I held up my hands. "All right, all right. I'll listen."

"Finally," Florry said, enunciating each syllable.

Getting up, I went back inside. Farrah, to my surprise —I worried that she'd been listening at the door—was sitting at the island, lost in thought, pen in hand.

"How does it go?" I asked.

"I wrote down all that I could remember. You really think this will help?"

I nodded. "No promises on what I'll find, but yes, I do."

"Okay," she said. Then she frowned. "It may not be possible for me to be here long if you're going to tell us that you're not interested in working with us."

"Your bosses can't have expected anything else," I said. "Tell them… tell them that you're working on me." I smiled.

"They're not going to buy it," Farrah stood up, pushing the notepad and pen away from her.

I took it, and as I did, I touched her hand. Light flashed in front of my eyes, and I heard the voice. Plaintive, afraid, on the edge of tears.

"Sure they will," I said, blinking. The voice continued in my head. "They were desperate enough to send you. I know what the former Oracle said to them. In detail," I added.

Farrah's expression didn't change, but I'd bet my best shoes she knew what Florry had said as well. "So they're tossing out a Hail Mary and hoping something will stick. Tell them you're trying," I shrugged.

I sounded like Florry not more than two minutes ago.

Where the heck had that come from?

"I'll try. And Wynter?"

"Yes?"

"Thank you," she said.

In her face, I could see the young girl who'd lost her mother. There was more to this than a mugging, or something like that.

I was going to find out exactly what it was that had taken a mother from a girl who even now, still needed her. Because then I'd have to tell her the truth about her mother. The truth that her mother was sharing right this moment, her eyes wide and pleading. Her mother had been scared and was scared still.

Somehow, I had to find a way to share this with Farrah. Seeing her, standing in front of me, I could tell she had no idea.

"Come and see me tomorrow. Tell your bosses you need some time to work with me," I said. That would give me time to think about how to tell her what I saw, and maybe, I'd have a chance to try to see a little more on my own.

Instinctively, I knew it wasn't going to be pretty.

CHAPTER EIGHT

While I really wanted to pull out my herbs and do a vision burning given the shade that was hanging around Farrah Lockwood, Florry was right. I needed to practice the magic part of this. Because though I hated to admit it, she was also right about me being nervous. If I could defend myself, then I would not have to depend on the Oracle traditions and the goodwill of people around me. Being more self-reliant would make me feel better.

I called Shelly as I walked out into the back yard, considering what to use. I put Farrah and her mom aside for the time being. "Hey, lady, what are you doing?"

"Whatever you want me to," she said.

"Can I try to send a pot to you?"

"Are you drinking?" Shelly sounded like she wasn't sure if she should laugh or be concerned.

"Sadly, no. I'm doing homework," I said.

At that, Shelly laughed. "And you thought you were done with school."

"Not even close."

"Okay, what do you need?" Shelly asked.

"Remember when I sent the stinky magic guy away?" I asked.

"Yes. I wish I could have seen it."

"Well, I need to practice. So I'm going to try to send a pot to you. Your backyard."

"Oh, that's kind of cool," Shelly said.

"I guess. Did you hear about what washed up on the beach?" I asked.

"No! What was it?"

I filled her in on the reappearance of the blond necromancer who had made an appearance again, and she gasped. "You think you—"

MAGIC & MENOPAUSE | 143

"I don't know," I cut her off. "But if I did, well, he would have killed me if he could."

"Of course it was self-defense," Shelly said. "Why are you sending me a pot?"

"Because if I break it, no one gets hurt."

"Well, unless you drop it on my head," Shelly replied.

"There is that. Okay, let me think about how I want to do this. It might be a bit. I need to see if there is anything in the grimoire that might help."

"What about Florry and Snaky?" Shelly refused to call Goldie by his name. She was mad at him; she said he should help me more, and she wasn't calling him his name until he did.

Unfortunately, as threats went, this hadn't moved Goldie to greater helpfulness.

"They both say I need to practice. That it will make me less nervous." I hated admitting this, even to Shelly.

"Well, it's a good point," she said.

"What? You think I'm nervous, too?" I couldn't believe it.

"You are. This is the first time in years that you're on your own, that you have to do things based on your own decision making, without worrying about anyone else."

"Wow. Everyone that knows me thinks I was a total doormat," I said. "Obviously my husband did, or he wouldn't have found himself another wife."

"Stop that," Shelly said. "Derek was weak. That's not on you. But you devoted your life to him, and the kids, and the business. Now, you get to focus on yourself. Which is something you haven't been able to do. Not only that, this is kind of dangerous. You haven't had any danger in your life… well… ever, Wyn."

"I'm not sure that makes me feel any better," I said, still smarting from her words.

"Change isn't easy even if you're looking for it. You weren't," Shelly said. "And you know I love you. So stop sulking and send me a pot. Just try not to hit me in the head with it," she added.

I couldn't help but laugh. "I make no promises about aim," I said.

"Whatever. I'll bill you if you hit me," she said. "Text me and let me know when you're sending it."

"All right. But I wasn't kidding—it may be thirty minutes or more."

"I'm not going anywhere today. You're not sending over Mr. Handsome, and I have no life, so... I'll just sit here and wait for pots to fall out of the sky."

We were both laughing when we hung up. That was Shelly's superpower. She never let me feel sorry for myself or get bogged down. Her motto was pretty much Carpe Diem, known as Seize the Day in English. It made sense she'd insist on the same for me.

"Okay, how to send this?" I thought about it and went out to the small shed in the back yard. Thankfully, I had extra terra-cotta pots. I brought out a couple of stacks of them, placing them in the center of the yard. I removed one from the stack closest to me, setting it further away from the rest. Then I went inside and brought the grimoire down from my room.

"Oh," I said out loud, looking around. I hurried to the door. I carefully locked and bolted the door. I didn't want anyone just walking in. Not that anyone should— but it's when you least want something that the some- thing happens. This way, I'd have a couple of seconds to gather myself.

Sitting back down at the island, I placed my hands on the grimoire. "Ladies, I could really use some help in how to guide your magic. I know everyone is different, but how do I... um... channel it so that it does what I want?" I sat with my hands in place for a minute, and then opened the book, hoping that someone would be willing to talk, as it were.

A ripple slid past the palms of my hands, light and gone before I could even articulate, much like a fish that brushed past your hand in a tide pool.

"Is that a sign?" I said out loud. I didn't move my hands.

Nothing happened.

"One step forward, one step back," I sighed, and pulled the book toward me to see if anything had appeared on the mostly blank pages. "Goldie? You got anything for me?"

Every Oracle has her own path to channel her magic, he said.

"Yes, yes. That's very clear," I rolled my eyes.

Just because you don't want to hear it doesn't make it any less true, Goldie countered. *Do you think you're the only Oracle who has struggled to find herself within the role?*

The idea stopped me in my internal complaint.

All of you struggle, Goldie continued. *That is one of the reasons that the Oracle is so unique within the world of magic. No two Oracles are the same. They both will help those seeking counsel, but no two Oracles will offer counsel in the same*

manner. It's the very thing that led the Oracle of Delphi priest-
esses to go underground and remove themselves from the world
of men. Being unique, being your own person, keeping your
own counsel in the face of strong opinion—that is not some-
thing that has always been seen in a positive light. He
stopped.

"This is hard," I said, part apology, part... I didn't
know. But Goldie's words made me feel like I'd been
whining.

Of course it is. Nothing worthwhile is easy. And Florry is right.
You, as the Oracle, hold a great deal of power. You need to
embrace that, to accept it. You are no longer Wynter Chastain,
mother and widow and whatever else you were. You are Wynter,
the Oracle of Theama. It would be good for you to remember that
at all times. You are fortunate. There is so much information
available to you, information that previous Oracles were not able
to access. Use it. Use the modern world for the good of the
Oracle, Wynter. There was a note in his voice that was at
odds with his 'go get 'em' speech.

"What is it, Goldie?" I asked, going off of nothing
more than a feeling.

It is nothing. Check the grimoire, and work on focusing your
magic.

Clearly, the subject was not up for discussion. I remembered, at that moment, that Goldie had been there

with all of the Oracles. All of them. And he'd seen things that were not great.

Perhaps this was something to look into, although not now. Right now, I had to focus on me, and making myself stronger. I opened the grimoire, slowly turning the pages. Nothing. Nothing. No—I stopped. The page in my hand was slowly showing words, and my heart sped up in anticipation. The page wasn't dated.

This is so hard. I cannot keep my focus, and I feel the weight of time pressing on me. Why can I not make this work? It's clear, both from my conversation with Lorena, and with the armband, that I am capable. But the skill comes and goes, and I am fearful that it will not be available when I need it most.

Two days later

I have done it! I have done it! I was able to freeze those who are hunting me with complete success tonight. That enabled me to leave my lodgings and take up the lodgings I have secured under a different name. I will share what helped with the focus for me.

I concentrated on seeing them frozen, on seeing them behind me, unable to move. That is the vision I saw in my mind's eye, and tonight, when I needed it, I made it happen.

Keep faith in yourself.

That was it. It wasn't signed, either, and to me, read like someone who was journaling so they didn't scream in public. Which I completely understood.

Okay. *Keep faith in yourself.* I did this once. And apparently I did it so well the person I sent away didn't come back. I didn't want that to happen again, my cocky words from earlier aside. What I wanted was to remove the threat from me and keep myself safe.

I pushed the grimoire back on the island, thinking. *Keep faith in yourself.* Visualize what you want to see. It sounded kind of new age-y, but, hey. I had a talking armband and a friendly neighborhood granny ghost. So I could no longer turn my nose up at the idea of a new age anything.

Getting up, I squared my shoulders, and went out in to the backyard. I quickly dialed Shelly.

"Hey," she answered on the first ring.

"I'm sending a pot your way," I said.

"All right. Where?"

Visualize. Visualize. "Near the bench along your back fence," I said. Shelly's fence had an open space behind it. It gave me a larger landing zone, so to speak.

"I'm heading inside, and I'll call when it shows up," Shelly said.

Clearly, she had no questions about my ability.

"Okay," I said, thinking about my best friend's assumptions. She assumed I would do it. That I could do it. There were no questions from her—and this was someone who had known me for years. Why? Because she knew I could do it.

"I can do this," I said. I put my phone back inside and then went out and stood in the backyard close to the pot I'd separated from the rest. "Go to Shelly's. On the back bench," I said.

The pot sat still.

I closed my eyes, picturing Shelly's yard, and then visualized the pot sitting in the middle of the back bench. Opening my eyes once more, I looked at the pot. "Time to go. Shelly's back bench, now."

The pot rattled on the ground and then it disappeared.

"Oh my god," I said. I'd done it. I'd sent it away. I ran for the phone.

Sent it to you I texted Shelly.

I know. It hit the door of the shed she texted.

Oh no. How's the door?

You can send tall dark n handsome over here to fix it LOL Shelly texted.

I laughed, part in humor and part in relief. Shelly loved any excuse to get Logan over to her house. But at least I hadn't broken anything.

My phone buzzed. **Try again** Shelly sent.

I put another pot in the middle of my yard. "Okay, it's your turn. Off you go. To Shelly's back bench." I saw the picture of the pot sitting on the bench in my mind.

The pot disappeared.

Sent I texted.

After a moment she replied. It hit the bench. I don't think it's fixable.

"Crap," I said.

Sorry I texted.

It's okay. Send another one.

I found I was nervous.

Maybe not hang out in the backyard I texted her.

I haven't been she texted back immediately.

I took another pot from the stack and set it in the middle of the yard. "Okay, on your way." I stopped talking. I didn't want to have to talk every time I sent something—or someone—away from me. *Go,* I thought. *Shelly's back bench.*

The pot disappeared. It was interesting how they just vanished. There was no pop, no flash of light, nothing dramatic like you'd see in the movies. It just wasn't there anymore.

The same thing had happened with the blond necromancer.

Sent I texted.

This time, Shelly didn't reply immediately.

I held my phone, waiting, feeling impatient.

What did I hit this time? I texted.

Nothing. It's not here.

That wasn't good. That was potentially how the necromancer had ended up in the middle of the Atlantic Ocean.

Sorry I texted.

Don't worry. Send another.

For the next hour, I kept sending pots to Shelly, until I only had two pots left. I was tired, but part of me was exhilarated. I'd managed to send all but two to her. Two of them, however, were goodness knows where. I hoped they wouldn't drop out of the sky and brain someone. Especially not Shelly.

I have an idea. I put an X on one of the pots. It's sitting in my birdbath. Try to bring it back Shelly texted.

What?

Try to bring it back now she texted. **You can't be just one way**.

I hadn't even thought about it. Why in the world would I want someone back I'd sent away. But it would be good to have the skill, I supposed.

My phone buzzed, and a picture came through in the messages. Shelly sent me a picture of the pot, with a large red X on it.

I stared at the picture, wanting the details to sink into my brain. Then I set the phone down and moved closer to the house. Although my aim had improved greatly over the last hour, I didn't want to be out in the middle of the yard and brain myself.

"Come back," I said, thinking of the pot. "Come back to the middle of the yard." I closed my eyes, breathing deeply.

Nothing happened.

"Come on," I said, feeling irritated. "Come back. Stop fooling around."

After a few moments, I turned back toward where I'd set my phone. **Did it disappear?**

It's gone! Shelly texted.

It's not here, I sent back.

I went inside to get a drink. While I stood at the sink, a loud crash reverberated in the garden. I ran back out to see a pot lying on its side near the fence. There was a fresh scar about two feet above it on the fence picket, but the pot on the ground was intact. I went over to look at it, and there was a large red X on the side.

I'd done it. I sent it away and brought it back.

"Yes!" I let out a whoop, pumping my fist in the air. Grinning, I set the pot down and twirled around my garden, arms out. Then I remembered I hadn't told Shelly.

It made it back I texted her and sent a picture of the pot. **I think I'm done though. I'm pooped.**

Hot damn Shelly replied. **I'm coming over, and I'll cook for you. Open some wine**.

I laughed, and carefully setting the pot on the back step, went in to wash my face and hands and open a bottle of wine.

Tonight, even with the shadow of my new consultant looming over me, I had something to celebrate.

Shelly not only came over and made me dinner, she cleaned up.

"I'm proud of you," she said as she was leaving.

"Oh?" I was pleased, but not sure why.

Shelly nodded, her face serious. "You've been hit with a lot in the last month. Derek, Natalie, Snaky, your old lady ghost—and you've managed it all. Now you can send pots wherever you want," she added, laughing. "I know you've been worried about this whole Oracle thing. But Wyn, I think you were made for this."

I didn't know what to say to that. I hugged her, and she left, blowing me a kiss at the door.

It was amazing to me that she'd say such a thing, but hadn't Logan and even Tethys been saying the same thing? I was the only one who seemed to be struggling with the idea.

I chose you, Goldie said quietly. *Everyone thinks that the armband goes to whoever finds it, but that's not the case. I must feel a connection with the potential Oracle. I felt it with you.*

"Why didn't you say so before?" I asked. I didn't bother getting mad. Piecemeal information was apparently part of the deal as the Oracle.

You weren't ready to hear it, he replied.

"Were you eavesdropping?" I asked. Since no one else was around, I preferred to speak to him out loud.

You did well with your magical practice, he said, ignoring my question. *Being able to bring something to you is an excellent skill. This will potentially make your future quests for your consultants easier.*

I hadn't considered that, but he was right. "I can just wish things to me?"

I don't know. It's worth trying. Maybe not in a life or death situation, Goldie said.

"Did you just make a joke?" I asked.

Goldie didn't reply.

"Okay, okay, sorry if I offended your dignity," I said, laughing a little. "I think I'm done with Oracle business for the night. I'm going to take a long bath and drink one last glass of wine. No eavesdropping!" I added.

I'll leave you to rest, Goldie sounded formal.

"Thank you. And thank you for what you said. I needed to hear it." I sighed. "You were probably right to wait until now."

I usually am, Goldie said quietly.

I could swear I heard a hint of laughter in his words.

CHAPTER NINE

The next morning, I called the apothecary to see the status of my order. I was going to need it. I didn't know how I knew, but I just knew. A young woman, not Nayla, answered the phone and informed me that the order was ready.

As I drove over, I found that I was cheerful, even as I wasn't looking forward to tell Farrah what I'd seen. No one wants to tell a kid, even one who is grown, that their mother was murdered, and from what I could see, was still scared to death. That suggested that whatever had killed her had something to do with magic. Otherwise, why would Mom still be scared? But I was pleased I'd been able to see her mother. I didn't know if that had more to do with me, or with Anipe.

Anipe may have died many years ago, but she was scared—whatever it was presented a threat to her daughter in the present day.

A sense of something far bigger than me came over me then. Thankfully, I was here, at the apothecary. I parked the car and leaned my head forward, closing my eyes and taking deep breaths. Something big was afoot. I felt it, like a shadow or a cloud had just surrounded me, chasing away my positive mood as though it had never even shown its face.

What did it mean?

I sat for a couple of minutes and then made myself go in. My cheerful mood was gone, and a sense of dread, like low grade nausea, was all that remained. As I put my hand on the door and walked in, I felt a flash of heat around my ankles.

"Oh, crap," I whispered. This was not the time for a hot flash, but I had no say in that.

I stepped inside, grateful for the cool air conditioning, and steadied myself against a display case near the door. The heat rose up into my knees, and my feeling of nausea increased. Was the nausea menopause, or the leftovers of whatever I'd felt in the car? I didn't know, but this just plain sucked.

The heat rose into my belly, and then moved to my chest. I knew from experience that once it reached my neck, I was going to be sweating like I was running in the middle of summer. Why had I even bothered to shower today? Good night, Maggie. This was ridiculous.

Sweat broke out over my forehead. I fumbled in my purse, now large enough to accommodate holding the grimoire, for some tissue, and mopped at my face.

"Can I help you?" a cheerful voice rang out behind me.

For Pete's sake. I turned around to find Nayla smiling at me.

She took one look at my face, sweating like mad, and probably as red as a lobster, and her eyes widened. "Oh my god. Are you all right?"

I managed to laugh. "No, not at the moment. I'm having the mother of all hot flashes. Could you get me a drink of water?"

She nodded and fled.

I must look even worse than I thought.

It seemed like a long time before Nayla returned, and she carried a red Solo cup of water. I took it, drinking it all down like I was at a drinking contest in college. When I finished, I could feel my hot flash fading. I used the tissue to dab at my face again. "Thank you," I said. "That one was really strong."

Nayla looked at me, and there was something in her gaze… something speculative. "I have your order, if you're up to coming back with me," she said.

"Sure," I took a breath, feeling myself return to normal temperature. "Thank you for putting it together."

"Of course," she said, and turned.

I followed her further into the store. Nayla led me to a door off to the side that had a sign over top of the door that said 'Stillroom'.

Once inside, she stepped around me, and pulled a curtain shut.

Which was odd, but I was overwhelmed once more, although not in a bad way, with all the fragrant herbs back here. It smelled wonderful, and I inhaled.

"Okay, what are you?" Nayla asked. Her cheery tone had disappeared, and the woman in front of me, hands on hips, was all business.

"I beg your pardon?" I asked.

"What are you? You were in the middle of something that wasn't just a hot flash when you came in. I could smell the magic."

I blinked. She said that like it was no big deal.

"The magic?" I asked, stalling for time. I was also stunned. I wasn't the only magical thing on the island? This sweet young lady in front of me, who looked to be of a similar age to my daughter Rachel, was magic as well? My head swam. Who else?

"Yes, the magic," Nayla said impatiently. "You are not someone who has ever shown any signs before, and now all of a sudden, you're in here ordering huge amounts of scrying herbs? We keep track," she added. "You've never been on our radar before." Her eyes narrowed.

"You need to back up and tell me what you're talking about," I said, drawing myself up. I was the Oracle. She might be suspicious but she didn't get to talk to me like this, even if she didn't know the whole truth. "Who is 'we' and why would I or anyone else be on your radar?"

Nayla took a step closer to me. "We are the coven on this island. We keep watch over the island, make sure that no one is doing things they shouldn't be doing. Ever since you came in here the first time, there is something alive on the island that none of us have felt before. The ocean is stirring," she said, her eyes blinking rapidly.

I wondered if this coven had felt the presence of Tethys. That was interesting. I also knew that whatever this coven was, I needed to make them allies, and fast.

"The ocean *is* stirring," I said. "Tethys is awake."

Her eyes widened then. "You know what's going on?"

"It's me," I said, deciding that I had to be honest. After all, I lived here, and I wasn't going anywhere. I didn't need magical people, regardless of whether they had skill or not, being suspicious or trying to make trouble for me. "I cannot tell you more, but what I can tell you is that I mean no one, not you, your coven, or anyone on the island any harm."

"You found the dead body that washed up yesterday," Nayla responded immediately.

"That doesn't mean anything other than I was in the wrong place at the wrong time," I said, unable to keep the crossness out of my tone. The hot flash was gone, but my irritation was still here, waiting for someone to pounce on and take a bite out of. Nayla might be the one today. "He would have been found by someone. I'm just glad it wasn't a kid."

"There is that," Nayla said, her expression neutral. Her hands were on her hips, and she didn't look any less serious. "What tried to come in here with you today? That wasn't just a hot flash."

"It was indeed a hot flash," I said. "The worst I've had so far. They're getting worse, too. You're right, though. There was something else. I don't know what it was. It was a sense, a feeling of foreboding. Like someone tossed a cloak over me," I added.

"Why?" Nayla asked.

"You got me," I said, taking a deep breath. "I wish I knew. Part of what I do is to help those who are seeking answers. I think it might be something to do with my current… seeker." I didn't want to say 'consultant'. Goldie said that a lot was known about the Oracle. If Nayla heard the word, she might put two and two together. I wasn't going to confirm or deny that I was the Oracle unless someone successfully did the fire ceremony and found me. Not even here, not even if I had to live with a coven that gave me side eye.

"What sort of coven are you?" I asked.

"Witches," Nayla said simply. "What else?"

"Oh, there are plenty of things," I said, thinking of all the magical beings I'd met. Did necromancers have covens? It would make sense if they did.

"Why can't you tell me more?" she asked.

"Because I can't," I said. "But I can promise you that I am not interested in harming anyone. My intentions are good."

"Will you swear to it?" Nayla asked.

"I will."

"With blood?" She whipped out a small knife from the pocket of the store apron she wore, extending her hand toward me.

I considered. "No," I said slowly. "I won't. I won't give anyone my blood."

Amazingly, Nayla's face relaxed, and she smiled. "That was the right answer, whether you knew it or not. Never give anyone your blood unless you trust them implicitly."

"I don't mean to offend you," I said quickly.

"You don't. If that was your instinct, it was correct."

I sighed, letting myself relax. I didn't feel like she was a potential enemy. Not that I had a built in bad guy detector.

She's not, Goldie said.

Thanks for letting me know, I replied to him. I meant it.

"So what are you doing?" Nayla asked.

"I am buying herbs for scrying," I said. "As I told you, I help people who come to me looking for help. Scrying is one of those things," I shrugged.

She continued to study me.

"Are you going to let me get my order?" I asked.

"I'm debating."

I raised an eyebrow at her.

"You sound like you take your responsibility seriously. So do I. So do we," Nayla said.

"Fair enough."

"There's nothing more you can tell me?"

"No," I said. "Not a single thing."

She considered me for a few more minutes.

This was getting awkward.

"All right," she said. "Let's go get your herbs. How is the burner working for you?" She turned, pushing the curtain out of the way, and walked back out into the main part of the store.

I felt like there had been a decision made, although I had no idea what it was. I followed her out. "The burner works. Better than I thought," I said.

"I have another one, one that's larger, and will allow you more access to the fumes," Nayla said. "If that's something you're interested in." She looked over her shoulder at me, and in her eyes I saw the gaze of another professional, as it were.

"I don't know if that's what I need, but I'm open to try it," I said. It might be just what I need. I was thinking about how to see more into what Farrah's mother was trying to show me. Getting Farrah closer to the burner might help.

"I'll add that to your order. How did you know about Tethys?" Nayla asked, not looking at me as she pulled a large bag from beneath the counter. She then moved along the counter, grabbing small things I couldn't see.

"She spoke to me," I said. I glanced around, but there was no one else in the store. It was surreal to be having this conversation, in the middle of Martha's Vineyard —but in a way, it was nice.

"What did she say?"

I smiled. "That's between her and I. But I can assure you, there is no harm meant by her words, or that she's communicating with me. More of a kick in the pants for me," I said, thinking about what Tethys had said.

"Sometimes we all need a kick in the pants. If anything changes, you need to let us know. Whatever it was that came with you today, it's still here," Nayla said. "I can feel it. It weighs heavy."

"It is," I sighed. "I don't know what it means, honestly. But if I think it's something that could be a problem, I'll let you know."

"Yes," Nayla said. "And Wynter?"

"Yes?"

"We can help you. I know that people hear the word 'witch' and think crazy cat ladies with crystals, but that's not the truth. If you need help, please ask." Her eyes bored into mine.

I reached out then and put my hand over hers. "Thank you. I mean that. If I need help, I will."

"Your word?" Nayla asked.

"I give you my word," I said.

"We don't need to know one another's secrets, but we take our responsibility seriously. So let me know if things go poorly," Nayla said again.

"I will," I said, my eyes meeting hers.

She nodded and rang up my order.

When I left the apothecary, I was feeling a bit bemused. My Oracle life and my regular life were colliding in ways I hadn't considered. Witches? Here? On Martha's Vineyard?

I called Shelly on the way home. "Did you know there is a coven of witches here?" I demanded without any greeting.

"I didn't know, but I'm not surprised," Shelly said. "We used to have the witch house, remember?"

"No," I said.

"It's fallen to bits now, but the story was that a farmer built his cottage, and in the process, got on the bad side of one of the local witches, and for the rest of the time anyone lived in the cottage, sand fell from the ceiling," Shelly said. Her tone took on an air of storytelling.

I remembered that she was on the local historical society committee and loved the island's history.

"But that's old news. I take it you're talking more recent doings?" Shelly asked.

"Yes. I went by the apothecary to pick up my scrying herbs, and the woman who has been making them for me asked me what was up."

"What did you tell her?"

I laughed then. "Not a lot, but I had to promise to tell her if danger was on the horizon."

"Not from you," Shelly said quickly.

"No, not from me, but who knows? My second consultant has a really unhappy ghost trailing around after her."

"Better you than me. When is Logan back? I would love to get him to tidy up my garden," Shelly said. "Too much pot isn't a good thing."

We both laughed. "I don't know," I said. "He had a list of things to do, and he said he was going to try to find a rental."

"I know of a couple who are getting ready to rent their places," Shelly said. "You send that man my way when he comes back. I'll get him sorted."

I laughed again. Shelly's Logan crush was over the top, but since both of them found it hilarious, I stayed out of it. "I bet you will, poor guy."

"What's on the agenda today?" Shelly asked.

"The new consultant comes back, and we talk. Scry maybe," I said.

"Okay. I'm around if you need me."

"Thanks, lady," I said.

When I got home, I felt better. The dark cloud, or whatever, was still lingering but I couldn't do anything about that right now. I was fairly certain it was Farrah related. My hot flash was a thing of the past, at least for today.

I called Farrah. She answered on the fourth ring.

"Hello?"

"Hi, Farrah, it's Wynter Chastain. I wondered if you might come over today."

"Okay. I'd planned on it. But you mean now?"

I nodded although I knew she couldn't see me. "Yes. Now, please."

"Okay. Be there shortly." She hung up.

Taking out the new burner that Nayla sold me—as if I had a choice, I thought—I filled it with my scrying herbs, and got my lighter ready. So far, I'd done most of my scrying and vision work on my own, but seeing Farrah's mom yesterday made me feel I needed to do this with Farrah.

And frankly, I wasn't looking forward to telling her what I saw. But it was the truth, and that was what she wanted.

Within half an hour, Farrah was ringing the doorbell. I let her in and led her to the kitchen.

"What are we doing?" Farrah asked, seeing my burner of herbs.

"We're going to scry, and see what I can discover for you," I said.

"What do I need to do?" she asked.

"Other than think about your mother, nothing," I said, lighting the herbs.

While they began to burn, I filled a pitcher with water, ice, and some lemons, limes, and orange slices, covered it, and brought the pitcher and two glasses over to the island where she sat. I found I was always thirsty when I finished scrying.

I knew what I was doing. I was delaying. This was the cloud that had followed me into the apothecary.

The truth.

When the herbs were burning well, a white plume of smoke rising from the burner, I sat down opposite Farrah, and pulled the burner closer to us both.

She gave a small cough.

I reached out. "Give me your hands."

Without a word, she put her hands in mine. I closed my eyes, and allowed the fumes of the herbs to envelop me, seeking the dark-haired woman who was clearly Farrah's mother that I'd seen when I touched her hand.

"Think about your mom," I murmured, looking for the woman in the cloud that I saw behind my closed eyes.

And then she was there, her hands waving, and her mouth open, clearly in a panic or some sort of state.

"Hey, hey, wait!" I said. I couldn't tell if I was talking out loud, or in my vision. "Slow down. I'm here to help! I want to help!"

The woman stopped and looked at me. Then a musical voice washed over me. "It's been so long since anyone could hear me."

"I hear you," I said. "Hang on, I want to share this." I concentrated, opening my eyes a smidge. Farrah was staring at me, her hands still in mine, her mouth slightly open. I nodded and closed my eyes once more. "Okay, let's talk," I said to the woman. "Who are you?"

"I am Anipe Lockwood, mother of Farrah, and the First Sister of the Sisters of the Asp." She said the name as Aa-nah-pee.

I repeated what she said, speaking slowly so that Farrah could hear me. "What do you want me to know?" I asked Anipe in the vision.

"I wish it were different, but my child is right. I was murdered. It was not a simple crime of happenstance. I was killed because I am the First Sister. Someone seeking the Fathers of the Desert killed me, to keep me from stopping them. To keep me from passing on the gift." Anipe's voice was sad.

I repeated all this to Farrah, taking my time. I felt her hands tighten in mine. "So by telling her the truth, I am fulfilling her quest?" I asked Anipe. It couldn't be this simple.

"No, daughter of the golden snake," Anipe said. "You need to help me. Help me pass the gift of the First Sister to my daughter and help her find the Sisters of the Asp. If you do not, the Fathers of the Desert will rise, and all will be lost."

"That sounds dreadful," I said before I could stop myself. "You want to back up a little, tell me exactly what's going on?"

Anipe gave me a mom look.

"Hey, I'm trying to share this with Farrah," I began.

"She is with you?" Anipe's face lit up. It was as though the sun had come out from behind a cloud.

"Yes," I said. "And I can share whatever you want me to share with her."

"Tell her I'm sorry. Tell her that I was training her for her role as the First Sister, but the allies of the Fathers found me, and ended my life. Tell her I've been with her always, and I am so proud of her," Anipe said. Her eyes glittered as though she were on the verge of tears.

As I talked with Anipe within the vision, I kept part of my focus for sharing her words with Farrah. Farrah's hands were sweaty in mine—and I didn't think this was coming from me this time, hot flashes notwithstanding.

"What are the Sisters of the Asp?" I asked.

"Long ago, the Sisters of the Asp worked alongside the Fathers of the Desert, to understand the mystery of the universe. To bring order to the universe. But power—particularly power that is akin to that of a god—corrupts. And so it happened with the Fathers of the Desert. There were eight of them, all men who served the Pharaoh. They were all brothers, these eight men. They, along with the Sisters of the Asp as their research partners, for lack of a better term," Anipe's eyes held amusement at the modern term in the ancient story, "Discovered that order of the universe was like a polished stone. There were facets of power that held life on this earth together. And when used together, balance was found."

"What are the facets?" I asked.

"That doesn't matter now. What matters is that there were eight known facets of power. And each brother came to hold control of one of the facets. Together, they were unstoppable." She shuddered, her face turning from me.

"The brothers argued with Pharaoh over how to rule Egypt, and he disagreed. It was they who sent the plagues to the Egyptians, they who forced Pharaoh to end the cruel treatment of the Israelites. Not because they were concerned for the people, but because they felt it was the wrong direction for Egypt. Pharaoh had no choice. He had to relent. And in that moment, when Pharaoh capitulated, the eight brothers became Pharaoh. Their power was absolute."

I didn't know what to say. This was mind blowing, when you thought about it.

Anipe continued, "When the Sisters of the Asp realized what the Fathers of the Desert, for that is how the eight brothers styled themselves, were doing, they broke with them. The Sisters knew of the facets of power, knew that each of the Fathers had taken a power for himself. So the Sisters devised a plan where they would divide into eight groups, and each group of Sisters would work to remove the power from one of the Fathers, and then lock them away."

"Did it work?" I asked.

"It did. It took many years, but the Sisters were able to strip the Fathers of their power, one by one, and hide the facets of power away. The Fathers were buried in a remote part of the desert, their tombs unmarked and hidden both by the sands of the desert and spells placed upon them by the Sisters. There is no good that comes of the Fathers of the Desert ever being allowed to exist again."

"Okay, what does this have to do with Farrah?" I asked.

"I am the First Sister, the keeper of the history, and the leader of those who stand against the facets of power ever coming to light in the human world once again. My death, and my inability to pass on my responsibility to my daughter, has allowed for those who have been seeking the facets to rise. They have found some of the facets of power."

"Who? Who is doing this?" Her words caused fear to rise in me. This was what I'd been feeling today. The rise of something with bad intentions. And I could tell that the Fathers of the Desert hadn't done a darn thing for the good of the people.

"Those who traffic with the dead," Anipe said.

"Necromancers," I said, immediately thinking of the dead blond man.

She nodded. "They have found six of the eight facets of power. The last two, the power of time and the power of will, have yet to be found by them. But they don't need to find both. With these two facets, if one is found, it will be possible to find the other. Whether by ordering time, or the force of will—the last of the facets of power will be discovered."

"And that means what for the rest of us?"

"Subjugation. Disaster. I cannot say, precisely. Until I was killed, the Sisters of the Asp were always there to hold back those who would resurrect the Fathers of the Desert. Did my mother, or my sister, not find my daughter? Why have they not contacted her?"

I said the last part aloud.

"They did," Farrah said, her hands gripping mine so tightly I feared for my blood flow. "They always looked at me like they were expecting something, but I had no idea what it was. And they never said anything! They never told me any of this!" Her voice rose, her anger evident.

"They could not," Anipe said as I relayed Farrah's words to her. "Only the First Sister can pass on the responsibility. You must find them. You must bring Momma and Panya here. You must. Only together can the Sisters hold off those who seek the facets!"

"Do you need to pass on the First Sister thing?" I asked within the vision. I could see that Anipe was upset and having a hard time focusing.

"Yes, yes I do," she said feverishly. "Have my daughter stand, and face the east, toward the rising of the sun."

I repeated this to Farrah, who let go of my hands. My vision of Anipe remained, however. That was good. I wasn't sure it would.

"Which way is east?" I heard Farrah mutter.

I pointed toward my back yard. "Are you facing east?" I asked, afraid to open my eyes.

"Yes," Farrah said. She sounded like she was clenching her teeth.

"She's ready," I said to Anipe.

The woman before me drew herself up, and a light shone behind her. I wanted to close my eyes, but they were already closed, so I turned my head slightly.

Her clothing, which until now had been nondescript, scrubs maybe, took on a different form, more of a flowing gown, in a light, airy white shade, and she held her hands out to the side.

"Oh Mother of us all," Anipe said. "I, Anipe, daughter of the Nile, the First Sister, willingly give my responsibility to my daughter, Farrah. I task her with the keeping of the Sisters of the Asp, and the protection against the Fathers of the Desert. I ask that my Sisters help my daughter, guide her for the betterment of all the Sisters and all that we protect."

The light around Anipe grew brighter, and I felt a rumbling, like what I imagined an earthquake would feel like. I felt myself stumble back and forth within the vision. I had no idea what I was doing in my kitchen and hoped I wouldn't fall on my face.

The light was so bright I could no longer look on it, and I shielded my eyes.

"Tell Farrah I love her," I heard as though from a distance.

Then I heard a cry close to me, and I thought it was Farrah. I opened my eyes then. Anipe, in her gown, the white light, the vision—it was all gone.

Farrah lay on the floor close to the sliding glass door.

"Farrah!" I cried out and kneeled down beside her. "Farrah!"

I patted her cheeks, turning her over to her side. That's what you did when someone passed out so they didn't throw up and choke. I wasn't sure if she would throw up, but since I wasn't feeling all that hot, I figured she might not be either.

"Farrah, wake up," I said, leaning down close to her.

She sputtered, and her eyes opened and shut rapidly. Then she sat up abruptly, bumping me in the forehead with her head.

"Ow!" I shouted, falling back while clutching my head. "Good gravy!" Today was apparently all about hot flashes and headaches.

"Mom? Mom! Where are you?" Farrah scrambled to her feet as she shouted, eyes wild as she scanned the room.

CHAPTER TEN

I wasn't able to get up right away, because my head hurt and I was seeing bright flashy bits when I blinked.

"Mom!" Farrah yelled, listing to one side as she walked into the living room, away from the kitchen.

I thought it was a good thing I had an open concept home. She would have walked straight into a wall—she wasn't focused on the here and now.

"Good grief," I said, getting to my feet. "Farrah! Honey, you have to sit down."

"Where is she?" Farrah was not the cool, composed woman who'd come into my house earlier. I could see tear tracks on her face, and her hair had come loose from the ponytail it had been in. It curled around her face. Her eyes were wide and moving rapidly.

Most interesting—or alarming, I wasn't sure which—Farrah glowed with a light that was similar to what I'd seen all around Anipe before I fell out of my vision.

"I saw her!" Farrah said. "She was dressed all in white, and she was smiling! Where did she go? What did you do with her?" She turned to me, and her eyes narrowed.

"I didn't do anything. She left," I said.

"No!" Farrah screamed. "Not again!"

You need to calm her, Goldie said. *She has just become a repository for a good deal of magic, and if you do not calm her, she's going to scream your house down.*

"Oh, hell," I said. Normally, I didn't swear much, but this was a rather extraordinary circumstance. *What do I do?* I thought, watching Farrah look around my living room for someone who wasn't there.

Slap her. She needs to reset. She's in between the worlds, and you need to get her back to this one.

You can tell that? I asked, fascinated despite the potential danger.

Yes, he said. *Stop dithering and slap her.*

I approached Farrah. "Honey, give me your hands."

"Will you take me to her?"

"Give me your hands," I said again, holding out mine.

She put her hands in mine, and then quicker than I thought I could move, I reached up and slapped her on the cheek, as hard as I could. I felt terrible doing this, but I figured I wouldn't get another chance, and if this was what it took to reset her, I needed to make the most of the moment.

Farrah staggered at the force of my slap, taking a couple of steps back, her hands dragging out of mine. She put her hand up to her cheek and looked down. Then she looked up at me, and I could see that whatever madness had been upon her was gone. "Ow. That hurts, a lot. What just happened?" she asked.

I sagged against the arm of the couch. "Oh my goodness. You're back."

"Did I go somewhere?"

"What do you remember?"

"I remember you telling me about some sisters, and a snake, and fathers, and then I saw my mom, and..." she shook her head, as though trying to clear it. "That's it. That's all I remember."

"Well, you got most of it," I said. "Let's get something to drink and regroup." I went back to the kitchen and poured us both a glass of water.

We stood together, and I thought about how to advise her next. Her mom had obviously passed on something to her, but I didn't really know what it was. "How do you feel?" I asked. "Any different?"

"I feel like I stuck my finger in a light socket, and I can't seem to settle down inside," Farrah said without any hesitation.

"Okay. So your mom did give you something."

"Like what? A disease?"

I shook my head. "No. She kept calling it the First Sister—hey, do you have the numbers of your mom's mother, or her sister?" I was thinking about what Anipe had said.

"Yes, but they may not want to hear from me," Farrah said. "I wasn't kidding when I told you yesterday that every time I saw them after Mom disappeared—" she stopped, looking stricken. "After Mom was killed," Farrah corrected herself, "They always looked disappointed."

"I think you need to call them," I said. "Your mom said they are part of the Sisters of the Asp—"

"What is that? And the thing about fathers?" Farrah interrupted.

"The Fathers of the Desert," I said, thinking. "She said your grandmother was part of this. So call them and let's see if we can't figure this out."

"You can't just vision up my mom again?" Farrah asked.

"I don't think so. I don't know why I say this," I said. "But I think she was waiting to pass this on. I saw her yesterday when I accidentally touched your hand." I reached over and put my hand on Farrah's arm.

Nothing.

"I don't see her anymore," I said. "She gave us the clues to follow. You need to get your family here. Or at least, on a video call."

"They're like the mahjong ladies my mom used to play with every month," Farrah muttered. "Older, judgmental, always giving the eye of disappointment."

"I'll bet they'll be glad to see you now. Tell them you saw your mom, and she passed the First Sister on to you. See what they say."

Farrah looked doubtful, but she refilled her water glass, and then walked out toward the backyard.

I let myself fall onto the couch. "Holy hello," I said out loud. "That was intense."

"You did well," Florry said from my right.

"You really need to come with a bell or something. If I wasn't so tired, I would have jumped out of my skin," I said, not moving.

She floated into my line of vision. "I tell you, I think you're going to be big doings as an Oracle, Wynter. I felt what you did. You helped a dead woman pass magic to a live one. Do you realize how hard that is?"

"No," I said honestly. "I'm glad I didn't blow up anything in the process."

"You're an excellent conduit."

"I'd like to be excellent at my own magic," I said, thinking about the pots earlier. "And to know what to do about the Martha's Vineyard coven."

"There are witches here? That's good," said Florry.

"Why? Their spokesperson wanted me to swear in blood I meant no one any harm."

"You didn't, did you?" Florry drifted closer, her expression one of horror.

"No," I shook my head. "I refused. She told me good job. But the threat was there, nonetheless. Don't start any trouble, 'cause we're watching you, that kind of thing."

"Did you tell them you're the Oracle?"

"No way," I said. "You only get that if you prove yourself. I'm not opening the door up for someone to find me."

"Good girl," Florry said. "How's your girl out there?"

"Shaken. I am, too. That was freaky, to put it mildly."

"Well, don't make any promises, and don't go off on her wild goose chase."

"I'm not done," I said, remembering Anipe's last words. "I thought if I helped Farrah find out the truth about her mother, that would be it. Anipe said no."

"Well, of course she would. You keep your own counsel. You'll know when you're done."

"What does that mean?"

Florry vanished as the sliding door slid open and Farrah came back inside. "They're coming here," she said.

"Who?" I asked.

"Nonna, my grandmother. And my aunt Panya. Nonna started yelling in Arabic to Panya, and then she said, Text me your address. We're coming. Then she hung up."

"Oh, lord," I said.

"Yeah, wait until you meet them. That's an understatement," Farrah said.

"Your mom said this has to happen," I said.

"Are you sure?"

I nodded. "I am, as much as I'm sure about anything."

"This is too much. I need to go back to my B&B. I'm going to call my boss, tell him you're a complete weirdo, and then I'm taking a nap. Nonna and Panya will be here tomorrow. I guess I better get them a room."

"That's probably a good idea," I said.

"Okay. I'll call you when they get here," she said. "I'm not facing them alone."

'They'll cling to you like barnacles,' Florry had said. She wasn't kidding.

"What time is it?" I asked. When I looked at the clock on the microwave, I was stunned. It was after five in the afternoon. Farrah had come here around noon. Now it was five? "That is definitely creepy," I said. "Where did all the time go? It didn't feel like we were scrying for that long."

"You're telling me," Farrah said. "I'm out of here. I'll call you tomorrow." She left without a backward glance, the door closing behind her with a click that sounded loud in the silence of my house.

I drank more water, made myself a sandwich, and went up to bed. I'd just fallen into a restless sleep when the doorbell began to ring, accompanied by a pounding on the door.

"What in the name of mother of Pearl?" I shouted as I dragged myself out of bed. A glance in the mirror as I left my room showed me that I was looking decidedly on the loopy side of things, but I also decided I didn't care. Let whoever was trying to break down my door get a view of me and all that my crazed appearance encompassed, I thought with a snicker.

"I'm coming!" I yelled as I made my way down the hallway. I yanked open both doors to find Scott Trenton with his hand raised and his finger attached to my doorbell. "You can stop ringing it now. I'm here," I said crossly. He didn't deserve any of my consideration at this point.

"We have an identification for the man you found on the beach," Scott said.

"Okay. And?" I asked rudely, crossing my arms.

"You want to do this here?" he asked.

"You're not welcome in my home," I said, remembering how I'd faced him down on the beach. "Since you're going to talk trash about me anyway, make insinuations, cast doubt on me, you might as well do it here, where it's all out in the open." I threw my arms wide.

A quick glance showed me that my neighbors, the Duffys, were out on their porch, and trying not to stare.

"It's all right," I called out. "Officer Trenton is just here to accuse me of dumping the dead man on the beach yesterday before I found him. You all are welcome to listen in."

The Duffys looked at one another, and then at me. "We know you had nothing to do with it, Wynter," Mrs. Duffy called back.

"You were saying?" I said to Scott Trenton, who was getting red in the face.

"As I was saying," he ground out, "We have an ID on him. His name is Jasper Huntingdon. Does that name mean anything to you?"

Other than the fact it would be nice to call him something other than the dead man, or blond necromancer, or as Logan called him, Stinky—I shook my head. "No. It doesn't. I told you, I don't know him."

"He was seen around here about a week or so before he showed up on the rocks," Scott said.

"Lots of people come here. We're a huge tourist attraction," I replied. "Does Andy know you're here?"

His cheeks got even more red, which I didn't think was possible.

"He doesn't, does he? He told you to leave me alone, didn't he?" I asked.

Scott Denton didn't say a word, didn't even move a muscle.

"You're not supposed to be here, which means what you're doing could be called harassment, Officer Trenton. We're done." I stepped back, slammed the door, and walked back upstairs to try to sleep.

This time, I had a smile on my face.

*T*he next morning, I felt like I'd been drinking when I got up. I was slow getting ready, and I had three cups of coffee before I felt something like normal again. I hadn't heard from Farrah, but I imagined she was probably not feeling so hot herself, and she was waiting on her family to arrive.

So I made lunch and then laid down on the couch to take a nap. I couldn't fall asleep though. What did this all mean, this Sisters of the Asp thing? What would I need to do to fulfill my part in this?

And why hadn't I heard from Logan? Knowing that he was dealing with shady characters made me nervous for him. I started to feel the worry rising in me, and I stopped it. Logan was a grown man, and a large panther to boot. He'd be able to take care of himself.

I needed to gird my loins for the arrival of what Farrah called 'the mahjong ladies'. I had no idea what that meant to her exactly, but I could picture my mother's bridge ladies, and if they were anything like the bridge ladies I'd grown up around, I understood her reluctance.

You never saw anything like my mother's bridge club. Those ladies were sharp, saw, heard, and knew everything, and were unafraid to talk about it, or tell you about themselves. I'd loved them to death because they were loyal to the end to both my mother and me, but they also scared the daylights out of me.

And I wasn't officially related to any of them.

After I'd been dozing on the couch for a while, my phone rang. The caller ID showed it as Restricted. That was probably Farrah.

"Hello?"

"Hi Wynter. I just met Nonna and Panya on the ferry and they'd like to come and see you. Would that be all right?"

"Sure," I said. "About ten minutes?"

"More like five," Farrah muttered, and ended the call.

I hurried to the bathroom to make sure I looked presentable and then cast an eye around the front rooms. Pretty tidy. I wouldn't be ashamed to have visitors.

Just as I was looking around once more, the doorbell rang.

When I opened the door, Farrah stood flanked by two older women. The older of the two wore a navy blue suit with a cream blouse, gold jewelry, and a creamy hijab. The younger of the two was in jeans, a red tee shirt, and a black suit jacket. Both were tall, beautiful, and reminded me not only of Farrah, but of Anipe.

"Come in," I said. "I'm Wynter Chastain."

"You are the Oracle of Theama?" the younger of the two women said as they walked in with Farrah.

"I am," I said. "Please, come in." I walked into the kitchen and waved at the chairs along the island. "Please sit down. May I offer you something to drink?"

"Tea would be lovely," the older woman said. She had a soft voice that was nevertheless commanding. She lifted her face up and delicately sniffed. "You were burning herbs. A good deal of them," she added, her English faintly accented.

"Farrah and I were scrying yesterday. That's how we saw Anipe," I said.

Both women tensed at the name.

"You saw her?" the younger woman said.

"Oh, stop for a sec," Farrah said. "Wynter, this is my grandmother Halima Emad, and my aunt Panya Emad."

"Call me Nonna," Halima said with a smile. "No one calls me Halima."

"Thank you for helping Anipe," Panya said, and while she also smiled, I could see her lips tremble.

"I didn't have anything to do with it. I was the conduit."

"What did Anipe say?"

"Can we at least sit before you begin the interrogation?" Farrah said. "And I'm supposed to be the cop," she muttered.

"You have bigger things to do now—" Panya begin. She stopped at a motion from her mother.

Everyone sat down while I made tea. The tension, the air of anticipation—it was so strong I could have picked it up and moved it around the room. But I didn't speak. No need for it yet.

Farrah looked uncomfortable.

Once all four of us had a cup, I spoke again. "Anipe said she was the First Sister, and she was killed because the Sisters of the Asp were in the way of people who wanted the facets, I think from the Fathers of the Desert? Do I have that right?"

Nonna and Panya exchanged a glance. It was Nonna who spoke. "You do. We are all that is left of the Sisterhood. After Anipe was killed, we were waiting for

Farrah to share that she'd been given the title of First Sister. It can only be handed from one First to the next," she smiled at her granddaughter.

That didn't seem to put Farrah at ease. She glanced away from her grandmother's loving expression.

Nonna continued, "But it didn't happen. Without a First Sister, we are weaker, more vulnerable. Over the years, the other fourteen women have died, or disappeared. Now we are all that is left."

Panya took her mother's hand.

"But now I understand. Anipe had been introducing you to the world of magic slowly. And she said that you always struggled with not telling your father. He is a good man, but this, he would not understand," Nonna said more to Farrah than to anyone else.

"No one, not even Mom, gave him a chance," Farrah shot back.

"She was bound to secrecy," Panya said. "We all take an oath of silence. We do not speak of this to others outside the Sisterhood."

"Wynter knows."

"As the Oracle, that is her right," Nonna said. "Wynter is also bound by the honor of the Oracle. She will not share your secrets."

"No, I don't share anything," I said. I had no idea if this was a thing, but I'd felt like this when Farrah asked me about my first consultant. I didn't want to share. I had no intention of telling Logan about Farrah. It made sense to me.

"Why can't we tell him now?" Farrah looked between the two ladies. "He misses her as much as I do," she said.

"We cannot," Panya said. Her words were firm, even as she looked at her niece. I could see that it hurt her to have to say it, to be so decided. But she said it. Panya didn't hesitate to do what it was she felt was her responsibility.

Farrah turned away. "This isn't right."

"Your father doesn't know about this side of our family history," Nonna said. "No one outside of the women of this family know. I didn't enjoy being unable to tell my husband the truth. It has ever been so." Her words were gentler than Panya's but Nonna was no less firm. "I am sorry, Farrah."

"I didn't agree to this!" Farrah whirled on her grand-mother and aunt. "I didn't agree to keep this from my dad, to never tell him the truth!"

I could hear the sharp pain of tears in Farrah's voice.

"But Anipe did," Nonna said. "She knew what was asked of a Sister, and what was expected of the First Sister. She has been with you all these years so that she might pass on the truth, her truth. Your heritage. Would you toss that all away?"

"Is there any way to tell the local police something? Something close to the truth, without telling the actual truth, so that Farrah's dad," I stopped, looking at Farrah. She'd never told me her father's name.

"Brian," Farrah said.

"So that Brian can have some closure? Not knowing what happened to your loved one is torture."

"We know this," Panya said. "We have also lived with this not knowing."

"But you were pretty sure it had something to do with the sisters thing." Farrah pounced on her grandmother and aunt. Unlike moments before, she'd corralled her emotions. She had on what I thought of as her work face—it was the expression she'd had when I met her, when she asked if the Oracle would help her employer.

"Dad doesn't have that. He has never had any idea what happened to her. It's like a wound that doesn't heal."

It was clear that Farrah wasn't only speaking of her dad.

"I am sorry. Truly," Nonna said. "I love your father. After I got over the shock of Anipe moving, and realized that we could still do the work we needed to even from a distance, I saw why she fell in love with him. He loved her very much. That was clear. Anipe was happy, happier than I'd ever seen her," the woman's face softened. "Yours was a happy home."

"Until it was ripped away."

"How would the truth help Brian?" Panya said. "It would cause him even more pain, to know that Anipe had a part of her life she didn't share. He doesn't deserve that, Farrah."

"Like you care," Farrah said, rolling her eyes.

"I do," Panya replied. "Mom's not lying. We grew to love your dad very much. How could we not, when we saw how happy they were together? And Sisters don't die like this—we have been safe in our secret for so long. The fact that someone knew what she was," Panya stopped, shaking her head. "It's dangerous to know. That's why Mom and I are the only two left. We're the only two who haven't been killed. Your mother died protecting you both."

"Panya!" Nonna said sharply, glaring at her daughter.

Panya closed her lips firmly and looked off out the window into the backyard.

"What do you mean?" Farrah caught on more quickly than I did. "What does that mean, she died protecting us both?"

No one spoke.

"What does that mean?" Farrah asked again, enunciating each syllable.

Nonna sighed, her head dropping. Then she looked up at Farrah, and her shoulders straightened, as though she'd made a decision. "Panya is right. Until your mother was killed, we Sisters lived out our lives in secret, in general peace. Our job, ever since Cleopatra—"

"Wait, Cleopatra was a Sister?" I interrupted, unable to help myself.

Nonna nodded. "Yes. And she was indiscreet. When she realized that, she killed herself, as was appropriate. She was a brilliant leader, a brilliant First Sister, but she talked too much. She nearly gave us away. Our success in our goal, keeping the tombs of the Fathers of the Desert sealed and hidden, and keeping the facets of power out of the hands of anyone who might use them, depends on those who might want the facets not knowing who we are." She sighed.

"We don't know how they found Ani," Panya said. "To this day, I can't tell you why they found her. She cast a cloaking spell on herself, and on you and Brian. To not only keep her identity hidden, but yours as well. She knew that being a Sister could put a target on you both, especially you, Farrah, if you showed any magical ability."

"Which you did, from an early age. Your mother worked hard to make sure that you didn't accidentally expose yourself, or her," Nonna smiled at her granddaughter.

Farrah didn't respond.

"She would call, telling us such stories. That you moved the cookie jar from the top of the fridge. That you pushed your plate away when you didn't care for dinner, all without moving a hand. You were strong even as a little girl," Nonna said.

"We helped her to devise a spell that kept others from seeing your abilities," Panya said.

"Including my dad," Farrah said.

"Yes, even him. No one could know. It wasn't safe. And that was before we lost the first of the Sisters," Panya said, her face twisting in pain. "Khepri, the next Sister to die, was found in her home, face down near her fireplace. There was no obvious sign of death, no sign of anyone forcing their way in, but we knew."

"We felt her passing as we felt your mother's. Not as strong, but we felt it," Nonna said. "At that time, it was concerning, but we couldn't be sure. We'd operated in secrecy for so long."

"Why?" I asked.

"Once we were the acolytes of the Fathers of the Desert. They worked at the behest of Pharaoh to solve mysteries for him, to help him bring order and balance to his people," Panya said.

"And we worked with them. Finding harmony and balance was pleasing to the gods, and allowed for the betterment of our people. But the Fathers found too much. They discovered the facets of power that allow for the balance of the universe, and that is when everything changed. They were consumed at the idea that eight aspects of power could rule everything. Over time, they grew to believe that they were of the gods, destined to find this power, and rule over all mankind," Nonna said.

"That is when the Sisters of the Asp broke with the Fathers of the Desert. We saw how it had corrupted them, how they used their power against Pharaoh, and worse, against the people they had taken an oath to help, to protect," Panya said. "That is when we knew we had to keep our identities a secret, that taking on the oath of the Sisterhood meant an oath of a lifetime, an oath of secrecy."

"And for nearly five thousand years, it's worked," Nonna took over from her daughter. "We have been able to keep the secret of the tombs, to keep the world from discovering the facets. We were able to keep their curse at bay."

"What curse?" Farrah asked.

"Where are the facets?" I asked at the same time. I kind of felt like they should have led with the whole curse thing.

"The facets were buried with the Fathers."

"What happened to the Fathers?" I continued. "And why is there a curse?"

"We killed them," Panya said, her eyes hard. "The Sisters of the Asp knew that these men would not stop.

Not even Pharaoh, who at the time was the representative of the gods on Earth, could stop them. If they no longer respected the chosen of the gods, they respected nothing. So the Sisters of the time killed them and sealed their bodies in tombs hidden in the desert. Nothing marked their passing. No pyramids or monuments marked their burial chamber. Only the Sisters knew, and we kept our secrets and our own counsel. When Khepri died, it shook all of us. We'd felt her death, and we knew that something wasn't right."

"Your mother increased the protection over you and Brian," Nonna said. "She was searching for who or what killed Khepri, and then..." her voice trailed off. "The curse," she looked at me, "Has been part of being a Sister of the Asp since that time. When the Fathers of the Desert realized what we were doing, one of them called down a curse on us. That we would pay for our betrayal and lose all that we valued. He was killed before he could utter anymore, but it was enough. That's why your mother worked so hard to keep you hidden, Farrah."

"We all hid," Panya said. "I don't know how they found Anipe, but we felt her die horribly," Panya continued. "All seventeen of us left at the time. We felt it. She cried out, and she fought. We felt her struggle. She didn't want to die, and she was angry, and afraid for you, Farrah. I felt the burst of magic she sent out, and I knew, because I knew my sister, that she was trying to protect you."

"It worked," Nonna said. "No one came after you. She cloaked you. They came for the Sisters of the Asp, and we have lost fifteen of our beloved Sisters. Someone hunts us to this day. But no one came for you, or your father. Your mother's last wish has been honored."

Farrah didn't say anything but tears fell unchecked down her face.

"I hate to be the specter at the feast," I said, "but won't whoever it is who has it in for you all be looking for Farrah now? I don't know the ritual or whatever, but I'm pretty sure that Anipe passed on the mantle of being the First Sister."

"What did you see?" Nonna turned her dark eyes to me.

I told them what I'd seen, and how Farrah didn't remember any of it, and that Farrah had a golden glow around her after I'd seen Anipe disappear into the light.

"That's what we felt," Nonna said to Panya. "We sensed a large burst of magic but we couldn't tell what it was," she looked at me. "It's been so long since there has been anyone other than the two of us," her head dropped.

"You accepted it from Anipe?" Panya said to Farrah.

"I guess?" Farrah looked unsure, and I was struck again at how young she was. She was older than my children but not by much. "I don't remember everything that Wynter does."

"She did, as far as I can tell," I said. "Although I don't know that there was much of a choice," I added.

"That is a problem," Nonna said. "This must be taken freely. No one is forced. To be part of this Sisterhood is a burden. No one is obligated."

"Do you want this?" I asked Farrah softly. "Your mother gave this to you, but you don't have to pick this up and carry it."

"Yes, I do," Farrah said. "Mom died for this. She died to keep me safe. I absolutely have to take this on." She took a breath and looked at her grandmother. "What do I need to do?"

CHAPTER ELEVEN

 I laid on my couch, blissfully alone, with a cold herbal compress on my face. Nonna, Panya, and Farrah had left about an hour ago, to go back to Farrah's B&B, and continue talking. I got the sense that they wanted to talk without me, and I was fine with that.

What in the name of all that was holy had I gotten myself into? The Sisters of the Asp? Whose members included Cleopatra, who killed herself out of dereliction of duty, if Nonna was to be believed? Who were fighting the ghosts of men who had the power to bring plagues to Egypt? I closed my eyes and inhaled deeply, letting the herbs of the compress wash over me.

It was almost too much. I had a monster headache, and while I wanted to make sure that I did my part, I was glad to be alone.

"I don't see how this is my responsibility," I said out loud. I wasn't sure who I was talking to.

"Well, I think you have to see this through." Florry's voice interrupted my calm.

"Were you hovering around listening to all that happened this afternoon?" I asked.

"Yes, indeed," Florry said. "This is some bananas doings, Wynter."

"Can't I just be done? I helped her find what happened to her mother. The mystery has been solved."

"What do you think? Does this feel finished to you?" Florry responded with a question.

"No," the word came out reluctantly. "No, it doesn't."

"There's your answer, toots."

"I was really hoping you'd tell me differently," I said.

"I was hoping you felt differently," Florry said. "I don't like this."

Nor do I, Goldie chimed in.

"Goldie isn't happy either," I said to the room at large. "They're coming back tomorrow to scry with me."

"At least those two can help protect you from whatever bad juju they're bringing."

"Have you ever heard of this facets of power thing?" I asked. "It sounds like something out of a movie."

The Egyptian priests were ahead of their time in regard to magic and the use of it, Goldie chimed in. *I'm not surprised.*

I repeated Goldie's words to Florry.

"Meddlers, is more like it," Florry sniffed. "Had they just minded their business, instead of going the route of take over the world, we'd all be a lot better off."

"Yes, well, while I agree, that doesn't really help," I said, massaging the space between my eyes through the compress. "The question is, what do I do?"

"When you have completed the quest for the consultant," Florry said. "You will know. You felt it with Logan, knew that you'd solved his quest, right?"

I nodded. I figured she could see me.

"Then you'll know here, and I want you to get as far away as possible from all this. It makes me nervous," Florry said.

"That's not good if it makes you nervous," I sat up then, the compress falling from my face. "I don't think I've ever seen you nervous."

"There's a reason why Egyptian curses are always the root of all the bad things in stories and movies," Florry said.

"What's the reason?" I asked.

"Because it's true." Her face was grim.

I laid back down, pulling the compress onto my eyes again. "Oh, mother of Pearl. What do I do?"

"Well, it's obvious," Florry didn't sound happy about it. "You have to help the Sisters get their bits in order, and stop the Fathers of the Desert, whoever they are." She snorted. "Who comes up with these names, I ask you? 'Fathers of the Desert' is about as pompous jackass as it comes."

"Absolute power corrupts absolutely," I said.

"Yes, and helping them is probably a good thing for your karma," Florry sighed. "Doesn't mean I have to like it."

"That makes three of us," I said, including her and Goldie in the 'not liking it' aspect.

"Wynter, you need to be careful. I have a bad feeling about this," Florry said.

"Message heard loud and clear," I said.

"Good. Don't you forget it. I know you feel for Farrah. But you can't change her past, or make that better for her. Her past is hers, and now that she's a Sister, or whatever—that's also hers."

"I hear you," I said.

"Good," she said again. "Goldie, keep our girl safe."

After a moment, I knew she'd gone.

Goldie, what was Caro's name? I thought. I found I was too tired to even speak.

What? He sounded startled.

Florry's human friend. She cared about her a lot. What was her last name?

She did care about her a lot, Goldie said. *I'm not sure this is something I should tell you, Wynter.*

I am, I thought. *Sure, I mean. You should tell me whatever you know.*

After a long moment, he said, *Her last name is Hackett. Carolyn Hackett. Are you sure you want to do this?*

Yes, I thought. *I've been thinking about it for a while, and it won't go away. According to you and Florry, that's a sign I should pay attention to.*

Yes, the one word was drawn out slowly, with great reluctance. *We have said that. But I'm not sure this will end the way you hope.*

What do you know? I asked suddenly.

I don't know what I know. I also go with instinct, and my instinct tells me that you are correct in pursuing this if it will not leave you be, but that it doesn't lead anywhere good.

You don't know that, I argued.

You're right. I don't. But I can't deny what I sense, he shot back.

"Fair enough," I said. "I need to do this."

Goldie didn't reply. That was his way of ending our conversations, to just stop talking.

I got up and put the compress into the sink. Then I went to my laptop.

Carolyn Hackett, also known as Caro, was easy to find. She was listed in the online directory. Her number was right there on the screen, just waiting for me.

Goldie's warning rang in my ears. Florry didn't remember how she'd died, just that she woke up in the in between. I wondered if that was because her memory, or something or someone was protecting her.

I carefully dialed the number.

"Hello?" a woman's voice answered.

"I'm looking for Carolyn Hackett, also known as Caro," I said. "My name is Wynter Chastain, and—."

Before I could get out another word, the woman on the other end of the call took a deep breath, and then burst into tears.

Oh, sweet baby Jee.

"Hello?" I asked. "I'm sorry, I didn't mean to upset you? Are you still there?"

She cried harder, and I heard her trying to say something, but it wasn't clear.

"Take your time," I said.

After a couple of minutes, she was able to speak, although her voice sounded wobbly. "I'm Caro. Only one person called me that."

I smiled. Figures. Florry liked nicknames.

"Are you the new one?" Caro asked.

"The new what?" I asked.

"Are you sporting a new bracelet, or tattoo these days?" Caro's voice was clearer.

"I am," I said.

"When they found her, he was gone," Caro said. "Like he hadn't been on her arm for over thirty years."

"How did you meet her?" I asked.

"By accident, but we became friends. She was the best friend of my entire life."

"She says the same about you," I said.

"You've talked to her?" Caro breathed.

"Yes," I said.

"What did she say happened?"

"She doesn't know," I said. "She said that she went to sleep and woke up in between."

"Florry was real worried that her time was coming. I kept telling her, You're crazy. You're as healthy as a horse, which is definitely suspect, given how much you smoke and drink. And then I go over one morning, and she's gone." Caro stopped, and the intake of breath that I heard told me she was crying again.

"I miss her," Caro got out.

"She misses you, too," I said.

"Good lord, I'm a waterworks," Caro said. "I'm sorry. I'm together now. I spent a long time with Florry. If you're calling me, there's a reason."

"How did she pass?" I asked. There was no easy way to ask this question, but since Florry couldn't remember, or didn't know, I had to.

"The coroner says it was natural causes. She was eighty-three, or eighty-four, I can't remember," Caro said. "But I don't buy it. She was healthy. I was with her at her last checkup. The doctor was astounded. She didn't take care of herself at all."

"What do you think it was?" I asked.

"I think," Caro said, her voice dropping, "That it was her last consultant."

"What?" I breathed. This was like my worst nightmare happening right before my eyes.

"She always had me sit in the next room, because she liked to have someone else hear from folks. She worried she'd forget something."

"As if," I said.

"My exact thought," Caro said, laughing now. It was a husky laugh, and I could hear the affection she'd had for Florry in it. "I thought she was nuts, but I did as she asked. He was very polite, spoke real nice. Like someone from overseas, who learned English after learning another language before. I peeked out. He was tall, good-looking, and blond."

My blood chilled. I didn't have very good luck with blond men lately.

"He told her he was seeking something that he'd lost, a piece of jewelry. Florry reared up then. He'd found her, which meant somehow he was worthy, but she was proud. 'I'm not a metal detector!' she told him. And then he laughed, and Wynter—can I call you Wynter?" she stopped the story to ask.

"Of course," I said, wanting her to continue.

"I've never heard a laugh that chilled me to the core like that. He said, no, you're not a metal detector, but you are the only person who can help me find this particular piece of jewelry. Then he stopped talking, and that made me look out again." She stopped.

"What did you see?"

"He was leaning over and whispering something. Florry was still, real still. It wasn't natural, if you know what I mean. I knew something was off. So I slipped out the back door, and came 'round to the front, knocking on the door and calling out, Yoo, hoo! Florry! Hey, girl, are you in there?"

Caro sighed. "Well, there was no answer, and the silence made my blood run cold, I can tell you. So I called out for her again, sticking my head in the door. It was just a screen door, because it was warm out. I stepped inside, and there was Florry, sitting in the chair where I'd seen her, staring off in the distance. I waved my hand in front of her face and then snapped my fingers right close to her. She blinked, and she was back again. She didn't remember him leaving."

"Why would he leave like that?" I asked.

"I don't know," Caro said. "I didn't see him again, because two days later, Florry was gone. I found her," her voice dropped in a small sob, and she stopped speaking.

I didn't say anything, just gave her the space to cry.

"I'm sorry. I'm not usually this leaky." Caro sounded like she was dabbing at her eyes.

"It's okay," I said. "I know you miss her."

"Like crazy," Caro agreed. "Once I realized that she was gone, I called the police, although it's only Ed Dumont here in Lost Springs, and he's lucky he can find his butt, frankly."

I laughed, I couldn't help it.

"It's not kind to speak ill of folks, but Ed is a poor choice. Anyway, Ed came over and shooed me out of the house. Doing an investigation, he said. Probably stealing Florry's cigarette stash is more like it," Caro made a sound of deep disgust. "I stayed until he was done and followed him back to the station. He didn't want to interview me, but I forced him."

"What did you tell him?" I asked. I found that I liked Caro, liked her a great deal. I could see why she and Florry were friends.

"Florry's cover story, a reasonable explanation as to why people were always showing up at her place, because Lost Springs is just a sneeze in the road," Caro said, "Was that she helped people with genealogy. Since that's what she told people, she actually did a bunch of work for folks in the area. She was good at it. I told Ed Dumont that I hadn't liked her last customer, and that he needed to look up Jasper Huntingdon and talk with—"

"What?" I breathed, nearly dropping the phone.

"Wynter? Wynter?" Caro called.

"What did you say his name was?" I asked, trying to calm my now racing heart.

"Jasper. Jasper Huntingdon. Real slick man, drove a dark black Porsche, and I told that Ed Dumont I didn't like the looks of him, but Ed being Ed, he didn't do a darn thing."

"And he was tall and blond and well-spoken?" I asked. I didn't know how I got the words out. My fingers were ice cold, and my heart was racing like I'd run a marathon.

What were the odds? First, he'd visited Florry, and then me? The only different between me and Florry was that I was still here.

"Yes. Wynter, what's wrong?"

"I have met him," I said slowly. "More than once."

"What?" Caro squawked. "Wynter, don't see him again. I don't know that he hurt Florry for sure, but there's no other reason I can find. She didn't die in her sleep. He did something to her, and I'll go to my own grave swearing it as loudly as I can. I don't have the same skills Florry did, but I know this like I know my own name. Stay away from him!"

"I don't have to worry about him anymore," I said. "Neither do you."

"Why?" Caro asked.

"Because he washed up on the beach a couple of days ago," I said. Good lord. Had it only been a couple of days? I felt a hundred years older than last week.

"He's dead?" Caro asked.

"Yes," I said, still feeling ice cold.

"Good," her response was quick, and I could feel her anger through the phone. "I can't prove anything, but he killed her. I doubt she was the first person he killed. I'm glad he's gone."

"What did he whisper to her?" I asked, thinking about what Caro had said.

"I'm sorry?" she asked.

"You said that he was whispering to her before you went out the back and came to the front door. Did you hear what he was whispering?"

"No," Caro said. "It didn't sound like English, though."

"Caro, I'm sorry that I called and upset you, but I appreciate you being so honest with me."

"It was my pleasure. It's nice to talk about Florry. And I'm delighted that blond good-for-nothing is dead. He killed my best friend, who was a good woman, who only wanted to help the people who came to her." Caro's voice was firm. "I'm glad to know that she's been avenged."

I wasn't sure about that, but something killed him. And he wasn't a good man, so he'd probably earned his bad karma. "I'm glad that gives you peace," I said.

"It doesn't, not really. But it's satisfying. And that's probably all I'm going to get. I'm glad you're safe from him," she said.

"He tried to kill me," I said.

"Well, then I'm doubly satisfied." She stopped. "Do you see her? Florry?"

"I do," I said. I thought I'd told her this, but at this point, I couldn't think straight. Jasper had killed Florry. He wanted Goldie, and he'd killed Florry. I wondered how Ashton Flint, my Indiana Jones would be midlife fling had found Goldie. He'd found him here. How had the armband gotten from Lost Springs, Kansas to Martha's Vineyard?

"Tell her, from me, that I miss her, the old bat. And that I'm going to live at least five more years since I'm not smelling her cigarettes anymore."

I couldn't help it. I started to laugh.

Caro laughed with me. "How I made it all these years, and her smoking like a chimney, I don't know. Tell her, too, that I drank a can of her nasty Olympia in her honor, and promptly donated the rest of that trash to Buzzy Chester."

"Will she know what that means?" I asked.

"Absolutely. She might even cuss," Caro said.

"You know, Caro," I said, struck by inspiration. "You can come out here to visit if you like." That wasn't like me, but I liked her. I liked how much she cared for Florry. And I thought she might be lonely.

"That's very kind of you," Caro said. "I'll have to think about it. I don't even know where you are."

"I'm in Massachusetts," I said, deferring to my own paranoia about people knowing where I was. I had to stifle a laugh, because it made me think of Logan and his asking me if I understood that his paranoia had kept him alive? I got it now.

"My stars. I've never been to New England. Well, that's a kind offer, Wynter, and I'll consider it. Is this a good number for you?"

"It is," I said.

"Let me think about it, and I'll get in touch. Will you tell Florry what I said?"

"Absolutely," I said.

"Thank you, dear. And thank you for calling to let me know."

"You're welcome," I said.

We ended the call, and I leaned back. Goldie had been right. I didn't like what I'd learned. Jasper had killed Florry. When Caro said his name, I knew that was what happened. He'd wanted the armband so badly that he killed for it, and he'd planned to kill me, too.

But why? Surely he, or whoever he was working with, had figured out that killing the Oracle wouldn't get them the armband? So why try it more than once?

I hated this. The puzzle was in front of me, and I couldn't see clearly. It was as though a mist was in front of me, clouding what I saw.

A mist. A mist that clouded vision, keeping me from seeing.

The memory of a mist falling on me, covering me.

"No," I breathed. Darn it. I wanted to stay here, and lie on my couch, and do nothing. I had a suspicion that tomorrow was going to be exhausting. I wanted to talk with Florry and see if she remembered Jasper the necromancer. My to do list was getting longer.

However, with this new idea, the latest item on the list had moved straight to the top.

CHAPTER TWELVE

*I*t was after ten in the evening when they arrived. I'd called Nayla, and asked her if her coven was able to sense curses, and if so, lift them. She'd been rather noncommittal on the phone, but had agreed to bring her coven to see me, to see if they could help.

I got the impression she was pleased to have a better look at me, and more importantly, allow her coven to get a look at me. I didn't like the idea of being inspected, but I was in my house, on my turf, so to speak.

If they got rid of the curse, I'd put up with it. Besides, it might be an act of good faith that would allow me to coexist with the Martha's Vineyard witches in peace.

I opened the door before they even set foot on my porch. Nayla was in the lead. I counted—there were six women of varying ages behind her. I didn't know any of them, which was odd. I'd lived here all my life. I checked myself. How much did I get out? How much had I done to get to know new people?

"Thank you for coming," I said as Nayla approached the front door.

"We're happy to help," she said, her face solemn. As the other six women came in behind her, Nayla added. "I mean that. We're happy to help."

"I didn't know who else to ask."

"What happened here?" The tallest woman had walked into the kitchen, and the living room, looking up and around.

"What do you mean?" I asked.

"There is a lot of residual magic here," the tall woman, who had a pale complexion and dark eyes, looked at me. "What are you? What have you been doing?"

"I gave Nayla my word, my bond," I added, "That I'm not doing anything that would harm another. I'm working to help people. One person. Well, two. That's what I'm doing. I can't tell you more."

"Can't, or won't?" Another woman spoke.

All the women wore dark clothing, and looking closer at them, all had on long silver necklaces with a crescent moon pendant. Most of the women had on other necklaces, although I didn't get a chance to really study them.

"Both," I said. "The things I am doing are not my own. I don't share business that isn't my own."

"That's fair," said the tall woman.

There were nods from some of the other women.

"Whatever you're doing, it's powerful. And untamed," the tall woman added. "I can feel it, straining to break free."

Her words made me shudder, thinking about what Nonna and Panya had said about the Fathers of the Desert and their facets of power. I still had no idea what those facets were, or if some of them were out in the wild. It also brought to mind Tethys' words. That my magic was wild.

"You do have a curse on you," a short, petite woman said. "It's sitting on you, like a toad on a rock."

I laughed, partly out of nerves, and partly at the image. "So it's not a nice curse," I said.

"Are any of them?" Nayla asked.

"I don't know. I don't really have a lot of experience with them."

"Any idea where you picked this one up?" the tall woman asked.

"I have a very good idea," I said grimly. "It was Ariadne, and her damn funky bull."

"What?" The petite woman gaped at me.

"You know the story of Ariadne and the bull?"

I saw a few nods.

"Well, she's real, and she's a pest. She thinks I have something she wants, and so when she couldn't scare it out of me, she showed up and put a curse, or a hex on me. I have no idea what it is, and honestly, calling Nayla was more inspiration than anything solid. But now that you've seen it," I nodded at the petite woman. "I'm pretty sure it was her."

"Why?" Nayla asked.

"Because she was spouting nonsense about me ruing the day, or something like that. She's bananas," I said, quoting Florry. "But I'm not an expert at removing curses, and I thought this might be more in your wheelhouse."

There was a silence, although it felt like there was a conversation happening that I wasn't privy to. Whatever was being said was not in harmony. I could feel it. The idea made me tense, and then I relaxed. I talked with Goldie silently. If the coven was chatting, that was fine.

"We can help you," Nayla said.

"Can you tell me what it is, too?" I asked. "I have no idea, okay, well, I think I have an idea."

"What do you think it is?" the petite woman asked.

I wished that Nayla would introduce me, so I at least had names, but I guess she felt this was better, so I didn't ask.

"Ariadne didn't speak English when it sounded like she threw the curse, but it felt like a mist, like a web," I said. "I looked her up, and she's associated with weaving. So it makes sense she'd use a curse that was similar to tossing a web over me." I made a face. "This is all conjecture, however. I have no idea what she did."

"We'll find out," Nayla said. She nodded, and all of the woman sprang into action.

They moved my couch back, as well as the coffee table and the two easy chairs so that there was an open space in the living room. From bags they pulled out candles, and bundles of herbs. One of the women was lighting the candles, and another placing the herbs in small shallow metal basins, and lighting them as well.

Then the lights went out, and the room was bathed in the glow of the candles. The light didn't reach the corners of the large room, giving the impression of a circle of light surrounded by a circle of darkness.

"Step inside the circle," the tall witch said to me.

I moved closer, within the ring of candles, and the tall witch drew me to the center. Then she stepped back, and all seven of the women stood in a circle around me in between the candles that had been placed.

Each woman stretched out her hands, clasping hands with the women on either side, and the tall woman began to chant. I didn't know what language it was, but it was melodious, and made me feel sleepy. I closed my eyes, even as I was dying to watch everything they did.

I could feel something swirling around me, and I forced myself to open my eyes.

A reddish mist was rising off of me. Off of me, drifting up toward the ceiling. Thin dark red tendrils waved in the mist, reminding me of sea grass I'd seen when snorkeling in the Caribbean.

I opened my mouth, but the tall woman held out her hand, effectively silencing me.

The red mist kept rising, and finally, it was off of, or out of, me, and hovering above us like a red cloud of insects. All seven women raised their arms, their eyes on the mist, and together they shouted something, again something I couldn't understand, and the mist burst into hundreds, maybe thousands, of little flames. Small explosions were happening all along the ceiling.

Oh, good grief. Please, sweet baby Jee, don't let my house catch on fire, I thought.

It won't, I heard Goldie's high, thin voice. *They're pretty good, these witches. This is not the fire that will burn mortal things, anyway.*

I hope so, I thought back. *You were right —*

I usually am. He interrupted me.

Stop with the self-congratulations. That cow Ariadne put a hex on me!

Whatever Goldie had been about to say was lost as the last of the red mist disappeared.

"That's that," said the tall woman. "The hex is gone. How do you feel?"

I opened my mouth to speak when there was a thud, and then I heard the clop-clop of hooves.

"Oh, no," I said, striding from the circle. "No, you don't. You take your behind right on out of here!"

Ariadne appeared, Stinky the Bull in tow.

Behind me, I heard a couple of gasps.

"Don't you have anything better to do?" I asked, completely exasperated.

"You have that which is mine," Ariadne said, looking like she was here to take tea. "When you give it to me, then I shall no longer be obliged to come here." She glanced around, her scorn skewering everything and everyone in my living room.

"It's not yours, and it never will be. We all know about you. All of us, through the years. You will never be what I am," I said, coming closer. I probably shouldn't be doing this, part of me thought, since I had to drag in witches to get her last hex off me, but I was too angry. "We share information, all of us. You've been plaguing us for years, and yet still, you have never been able to get the thing you wanted. You ever wonder why?"

"You dare to speak to a goddess this way?"

"A goddess my aunt Fanny!" I laughed. "If you're a goddess, you're a sorry representation of one. You cannot have it, Ariadne. It chooses who will have the honor, and you will never be chosen."

"You're not a seer," she said. Her voice was still calm, but I sensed a crack in her calm façade.

"I don't need to be. You're not mortal. You have no sense of helping others. That's what this is—a lifetime gig of helping others," I said, thinking how much I sounded like Florry. "And you don't have what it takes to take on such a responsibility. Now get out of my house and take bad breath over there with you. He's steaming up my windows." I gestured at the bull who I could smell from here.

How in the name of all that was decent did she put up with the smell? And if he was some kind of immortal, how come he still smelled so bad? God.

"Or what?" Ariadne asked. "You'll put your witches on me?" She lifted her chin toward the women who stood silently behind me.

"I don't need them to handle you," I said. I took my anger, no, my rage, and I channeled it into one single thought. Go away and never return. Where did I want her to go? To a dark cave, on Crete, and be stuck there with the bull.

Go away, I thought. *Go away to the cave. Go away.*

Ariadne's eyes widened and her hands flew out attempting to ward off something she couldn't see.

Welcome to the club, honey, I thought.

"What are you doing?" Ariadne screamed.

I didn't respond. This was harder than I imagined. Both Ariadne and the bull were strong magical presences. I closed my eyes and saw the cave, and saw them there, unable to leave.

Go, I thought. *Get away from me, you pain in the butt.*

Ariadne let out a scream that rattled my bones. I'd heard the expression before, but I'd never experienced it. If this was what it was like, I didn't want to ever experience it again. Ever.

Holy hello.

Ariadne screamed again, and I covered my ears and thought, *Go! Just go! Never return!*

Then the scream ended, and the room was calm once more. Well, relatively speaking as far as calm.

The witches around me were silent and then one started to laugh. "I have no idea what just happened, but that was comeuppance in action," she got out, and laughed harder, bending over as she did so.

Nayla smiled at me.

"What was the curse?" I asked as another witch joined the first woman laughing.

The tall woman, who was smiling as she watched her sisters, looked down at me. "Essentially, it was a confusion curse. She made it hard for you to see clearly. It was kind of a mess, though. A lot of anger, and extra pieces that didn't need to be there."

"I don't know that curses are really her thing," I said. Was I apologizing for the muzzy headedness of that wretched woman? What was wrong with me?

Nayla laughed. "It was a mess, but it was effective. You should be more clear eyed now."

"Thank you for coming over to help me," I said.

"It was our pleasure," the tall witch said. "After speaking with Nayla, we were interested to meet you."

"Likewise," I said.

"What of the matter you and Ariadne spoke of?" The petite woman who had spoken to me before asked.

"That is between us," I said, trying not to get huffy.

The tall witch waved a hand. "We can see that. And we will hold you to your word that you are not intending harm upon others. I have to ask, though— what did you do with Ariadne?"

"I sent her back to Crete," I said. "That was my goal, anyway." I shrugged. I had no idea if I'd done it, but that was my intention. "In one piece," I added.

Several of the women laughed.

"You're curse free now," the tall witch said. "Please don't hesitate to get in touch with Nayla if you need any more help."

"How can I thank you?" I asked. I meant it. I owed them. I didn't like the idea of no reciprocity with people who'd done me a pretty big favor.

"Nayla says that you scry," the tall witch said.

She must be the leader, I thought. She spoke like a leader, and all of the women seemed to take their lead from her.

"I do," I said. "Although I wouldn't call myself an expert."

"Well, I'll ask that you help us scry at a future date, if that's agreeable to you," the tall woman said.

"Of course," I said.

"Then we're agreed," the tall witch said. "Ladies, we're done." She nodded at me and walked toward the hallway.

The other six women, including Nayla, gathered the candles and the basins with the burned herbs, placing them in a reusable grocery bag. Then with solemn nods, they left.

Nayla was last. "I'm glad you called me, Wynter. There's room for all of us to keep our own counsel, but we have to be able to trust one another."

"I trust you," I said. I meant it.

"I think we can trust you as well," she said, smiling. "Good night. I hope this helps you rest easier."

"It will," I said. Damn that Ariadne. Hopefully, I'd gotten her out of my hair and made her think twice about bothering me again.

The door closed behind Nayla, and I was alone. I went back to the kitchen and made myself a cup of tea, thinking about all I'd learned this day. While having the witches remove the curse from me had taken up my evening, I couldn't stop thinking about what I'd learned earlier. The question was, did I tell Florry?

Yes, Goldie said. *You must.*

"It's going to break her heart," I said.

You don't know that. You cannot take the truth from people, Wynter. That's one of the things that we all deserve, even when painful.

"Is it?" I asked. "Is it better to tell her this?"

Yes, he said. There was no hesitation in his reply.

"Lord help us all," I said. "Florry? Are you around?" I waited, hoping that for once, she did her no show thing.

No such luck.

"What's up?" Florry appeared in the vicinity of the fireplace.

I sighed. "I talked to Caro today." I watched her face carefully.

"How is she?" Florry's face tightened.

"She misses you," I said. "I invited her to come here, if she wants. She also wants you to know that she drank an Olympia in your honor and then gave the rest to Buzzy Something-or-other."

Florry started to laugh. "He's probably still drunk," she got out before she dissolved in gales of laughter.

I was glad to see her laugh, even as I didn't want to tell her the rest.

You must, Goldie said.

Yeah, yeah, I thought. *I know*.

"What else did Caro say?"

"She knows how you died," I said, deciding to just get it out there. Florry's brusqueness was rubbing off on me.

Florry drifted closer, and I could see her eyebrows reaching for her hairline. "Oh?"

Well. That was decidedly neutral.

"Yes," I said. "Do you remember the blond necromancer? His name is Jasper. Do you remember meeting him?"

Florry frowned. "Sort of."

"He… oh, god. There's no easy way to say this. He killed you, Florry. Caro said she couldn't prove it, but she says that you didn't die of natural causes." I felt the ache in the back of my throat and the welling of tears in my eyes.

"That sonofabitch," Florry said conversationally. "I'm glad you sent him to Timbuktu, or wherever you sent him, Wynter. Because whatever happened after that, someone dumped him over the side of a boat, and sounds like he earned it. Why? Why kill me?"

She was taking this better than I thought. "I think he wanted Goldie."

"I thought most of the supernatural world understood that the armband chooses the Oracle, not the other way around," Florry rolled her eyes and lit a cigarette.

"Apparently not," I said. "Ariadne's been not getting the message for how many centuries? That's not the point, Florry. I'm so sorry."

"Why?" she asked again. "You can't count Ariadne as anything. She's a wannabe goddess with an obsession. That's not normal."

"Because I didn't want to tell you this," I said.

"It's facts, toots. I died. You're going to die one day. We all do. Let me guess. Caro found me?"

I nodded.

"Poor Caro. No one should have to find their friend that way," Florry said. "I'm glad you invited her out here. What did she say?"

"That she'd think about it," I said.

"Oh, no. That means 'no' in Caro-speak. You need to call her back and tell her I said that she has three months to get her poop in a pile, and come visit you. She doesn't have anyone else. She and I were it for each other, so she needs to get some of that found family I was always reading about."

"She may not want it," I said.

"Horse manure. We all want a family. You tell her what I said."

"All right," I sighed. "I'll call her tomorrow."

"And you tell her what I said. Exactly." Florry gestured with her cigarette.

"Exactly," I said, giving her a mock salute. "I think I need to go to bed now, however. Farrah and her mahjong ladies are coming over tomorrow, and we're going to scry together, to see where these facets are, or something," I said. "I'm not quite clear on what we're doing, exactly, but I wasn't going to be the one who told Nonna that fact."

"No, she's the kind you just say, Yes, ma'am to," Florry said. "And Wynter?"

"Yes?"

"Thank you. For calling Caro, and for finding the truth of my end. It's a comfort to know."

"Really? I didn't think you'd find it very comforting."

"I was kind of worried that I couldn't remember, and I didn't know if that was normal. I don't have the grimoire anymore, and I can't call for Patsy specifically, so…" she shrugged. "I was kind of in the dark. That's one place I don't care to be."

"Well, now you know."

"It helps to know that the person who did this is deader than a doornail," Florry said. "Not going to lie, it definitely helps. I might be a bit more salty if he was still walking around."

I laughed. I couldn't help it. Her response was so Florry.

"Anything else?" Florry said.

I gave her the abbreviated version of what had happened with the witches.

"That was a good call, asking for their help. Now they feel like they know something about you, which makes them less suspicious. And asking to scry with you isn't all that demanding."

"Says you," I said. "I'm on the verge of a hot flash at all times, and the idea alone makes me sweat. I don't ever want to wear a bra again, and every time I scry, it wrings me out like a sorry dishcloth."

"Whine, moan, carry on," Florry said. "These are first world problems, even as the Oracle. You should go to bed," she added.

"I was planning on it."

"All right. I'll keep an eye out on you tomorrow, make sure the Asp Sisters don't get you an asp in a basket," she said.

"You have such great faith in your fellow man," I said.

"Nope. Just realistic. People love nothing more than sharing their misery," Florry said cheerfully.

"That's my cue," I said, getting up and putting my cup in the sink. "I'll see you tomorrow."

"Wynter?" Florry said.

"What?" I turned, one foot on the stairs.

"Thank you."

I smiled. "My pleasure, toots."

Her chuckle followed me up the stairs. I fell asleep with a smile on my face. Today had been a good day, overall.

CHAPTER THIRTEEN

When I got a text from Farrah, I was already up, ready to start brewing tea, and I had snacks. Lemon bars and cookies. I also made some chicken salad, because I had a feeling today was not only going to be a long day, but draining. Cooking soothed me.

My bosses are calling you a number of creative names. Just in case you are feeling a strong sense of irritated focus in your direction Farrah texted.

Life is full of disappointments. I'm ready whenever you want to come over I texted back

LOL was her response. **On our way.**

While I was waiting, I called Shelly.

"What's up?"

"I'm involved with my new consultant all day. If you don't hear from me by tomorrow, come over and use the key to see what is going on."

"Are you in danger?" she asked.

One thing I loved about Shelly was that she didn't get all dramatic. Rather she did what needed doing at the time and then yelled at me later to vent her worry. This had been her manner even before I became the Oracle.

"I've had nothing but danger since I got Goldie, so nothing out of the ordinary. I'm just not sure what to expect today," I said.

"You got it. Where's that handsome man?" she asked.

"He's not back," I said. "I kind of expected to hear from him before now, but it's not like he needs to check in or anything."

"Uh huh," Shelly said. "Whatever you have to tell yourself. Good luck today. I'll check in tomorrow."

"Thanks, Shell."

"No problem."

I felt better giving someone an idea of what was going with me. Just as I'd leave a float plan with someone if I went out on the water. Shortly after I spoke with Shelly, the doorbell rang and Farrah and her family came in.

I'd already prepped all my scrying supplies. "I just need to know what the goal is today," I said. "I feel like I'm not really clear on everything."

"We need to see where the facets are," Panya said. "As Mom told you, there are eight. Six of them have been found."

"We need to know where the first and eighth facets are," Nonna said.

"Why?" I asked.

"Because the first facet, the power of time, allows the holder to order time to do whatever they need. With the first facet, they can get the eighth facet without any trouble. Same with the eighth facet—the power of will allows the bearer to order things to their will, so they can find the first facet easily. And with all eight facets, the bearers can open the tombs of the Fathers of the Desert." Panya was the one who answered.

I kind of thought they'd touched on this yesterday, but I needed to hear it again. "Thank you," I said. "What are the other facets?" I asked.

"Air, earth, water, fire, dreams, and death. With these things, the tangible and intangible aspects of life, all things are possible."

"What's the point of all this?" I asked.

"Well, when the Fathers of the Desert were able to obtain the facets of power, they were able to live a life of indulgence and debauchery. They did what they wanted. There were no limits, no consequences. And they loved it," Nonna said. "The Sisters of that time were appalled, and that's when they began to work to separate all the Fathers from the facets. It took them over a year to set things up, and then they moved on the Fathers all at once."

"It's been a fight ever since. Even entombed and dead, the eight brothers are strong magic users," Panya said. "They have not been at peace in their afterlife." Her eyes rolled.

"How are you?" I looked at Farrah. "You've been quiet."

"I don't know what to think," Farrah said. "I have to be the First Sister, and I don't know how to be her. It. Whatever."

"I think that's why you're here," Nonna said to me. "I mean, involved in this. Because of you, Ani was able to pass the power of the First Sister to Farrah, but she cannot just take on the role without help. I think you're here to help Ani connect with Farrah so that Farrah can do this on her own."

I watched Farrah while her grandmother spoke. Her shoulders hunched up around her ears, and she hugged herself tightly. This wasn't someone who was thrilled at what was about to happen.

"Are you sure you want to do this?" I asked Farrah.

Panya made a noise of anger, cut off abruptly by her mother. I ignored her. My concern was Farrah, my consultant. No one else.

"I don't have a choice," Farrah said. "My mom died for this, and she stayed around so that she could pass this on to me. I have to do it," she said, looking at me earnestly. "I know it seems like I'm being pushed, and maybe I am, but I couldn't live with myself if things went badly because I didn't want to take it on."

I understood that, as much as I wanted to hug her and tell her she didn't have to do this. "If you're sure," I said.

"I am," Farrah said. "Not thrilled, but I don't have any doubts."

"This isn't your place to question," Panya said, her voice low and angry.

"Oh, but it is. My responsibility is to my consultant. Not to you, or your goal, or anything else. Farrah is my responsibility." I gave Panya eyeball for eyeball.

Maybe being around Florry was good for me. I was standing up for myself against people that I personally found intimidating, and I wasn't even nervous to stand up to them.

Because I was right. Righteousness made me strong.

Careful you don't get too righteous, Goldie whispered.

I'm not, I said. *I just hate seeing anyone pushed around by their stronger family members. Farrah is strong, so to me, that tells me what she's up against.*

She's made her choice, Goldie said.

I know, I said. *I needed to be sure.*

That's not a bad thing, but don't alienate the Sisters of the Asp. We need them. You need to help them. The Fathers of the Desert would unleash a hell on this earth the likes of which you've never seen.

You're familiar with them? I asked, astounded.

I am. *The cause of the Sisters of the Asp is a noble one*, he replied.

All three of the women were staring at me, and I blinked. "Sorry. I was… well, it doesn't matter. I sometimes have those no one else can see communicate with me."

Nonna peered around. "Really? Who's here?"

"That's not important to anyone but me," I said. "Sorry I spaced for a moment. So. We're scrying, then? What are we looking for exactly?"

"Any of the symbols of the Fathers of the Desert. We know what to look for," Panya said quickly.

"Then why do you need me?" I asked.

"Because there is a reason Anipe showed herself to you. While we cannot see what that is, she had a reason," Nonna said.

Hmm. That wasn't really a great answer, but looking at Nonna and Panya, it was clear that was the only answer I would be given.

"All right. Let me get the herbs going," I said. I lit the larger basin I'd gotten when I got my large bulk order of herbs. I figured with four of us, and the extent of what the Sisters of the Asp wanted, we'd need it.

As the smoke began to form over the basin, I came to stand next to Farrah. "Take my hands," I said. "Nonna, Panya, place your hands on mine and Farrah's." I knew that it was important that Farrah and I kept direct contact, but I also needed to touch the other ladies, to focus on searching for the facets that they were familiar with.

Everyone stood in a small circle, the smoke from the herbs getting thicker, surrounding us. "Close your eyes and breathe deep. I want Nonna and Panya to focus on what we're supposed to be looking for, and Farrah, focus on your mom."

The room was quiet, and I let my mind open up. It was like visualizing a flower opening, one petal at a time, exposing more and more. I wanted to be available to see anything that wanted to be seen. No matter what.

A voice whispered into my ear. It wasn't Goldie, Florry, or any of the ladies with me. I listened. "Farrah," I spoke softly. "Let your mind open and see what it is that your gran and aunt see. We need to see the symbols of the Father of the Desert. That will lead us to those who seek their power."

On my right, I felt Panya startle. She didn't expect me to know this. I realized in that moment she didn't expect much of the scrying.

Why were people constantly underestimating me?

Farrah's breath caught, and her hands jerked in mine. I guessed that she was seeing something from her gran or aunt. I didn't say anything more, just waited.

To the left, Nonna gasped.

What does she see? I thought. *Show me.*

My vision remained black. But then I saw a swirling in the distance, like gray fabric moving in a circular fashion. I focused on the movement of the drapes, or whatever it was. The movement got closer, more in focus.

As it came closer to where I could see, the gray disappeared and I saw a group of men. They were dressed in the robes of what I guessed were ancient Egypt, because it wasn't what the men on the Vineyard were wearing, and men around here made some questionable choice. The men were arguing.

"… we must stop them," one of the men said, his face red and his jaw tight.

"We cannot," another man said. "They have planned this well."

"But they will not escape the consequences of their actions," a third man said. This one gazed beyond the men he was with, and I felt like he was looking right at me. It was seriously uncomfortable.

I felt a warmth around my ankles. Sweet baby Jee, not now. This was not the time for a hot flash.

As the man in the vision continued to stare at me, I felt the heat rising up my legs.

"Women are not as capable as men," the man said, his eyes boring into mine. "They think they are, but they aren't. In the end, we shall triumph. We need but be patient, my brothers." He looked to the men around him. "We shall triumph."

A golden sunburst—there was no other way to describe it—formed over the man's head. Not the actual sun, but like something golden and bright glowing over his head.

What was it? I tried to peer more closely, but it was hard. Whatever it was, it got brighter and brighter.

I squinted, trying to see what it was.

It was a seal, or at least, that's what it looked like to me. Gold, with blue... blue enamel between the gold lines. It was in the shape of a dog's head with a headdress— the god Anubis, I thought. How I knew that, I had no idea.

Without thinking about it, I reached for the seal. The man who had made eye contact with me looked at me again and smiled. There was no humor, or light, or anything positive in his smile. He reminded me of an animal coming in for the kill. "You may take it, but it will offer you no help," he said.

My fingers closed around the seal.

"I warned you," the man said.

The vision went black, and I felt myself fall back. I opened my eyes to find myself on the floor, my right hand clenched around something. "Holy hello," I said.

"What do you have?" Farrah asked.

I got up and opened my hand. The blue and gold seal floated free, a golden glow around the seal.

"The power of death," Panya gasped. "They have it."

Wind rose in my living room, and as the wind grew stronger, I could feel the grit of sand whirling around me. "Who has it?" I called out. "Don't we have it? Right here, in my hand?"

"What is going on?" Farrah shouted.

"Take my hand!" Nonna yelled.

I had no idea who she was talking to. I reached for her, but before I could, the sand and grit solidified in front of me, a small sand tornado in my house.

This is never going to come out of my carpet or couch, I thought absently.

The seal still floated above my hand. I couldn't look away from the seal. It was beautiful, and deadly, and all I wanted was to hold it, keep it close. My hand moved up to take it once more.

"No," a man's voice said. "I don't think so. Not even a First Sister can help you now."

The sand in front of me took on more of a form, and then out of the sand stepped Tomas Severn.

"You!" I gasped. My fingers tried to reach the seal, but it hovered just out of my grasp.

"Have we met?" Tomas peered at me. Then he shook his head. "It doesn't matter. This is not for you. How did you even come by it?" His head tilted, a bird watching its prey.

"That's not your concern. This is not for you, either."

"I don't think you know what you're talking about," Tomas smiled. He gazed around at the other women. "Pathetic. Her giving the power away won't help you."

He looked down at me again. "You could join the winning side, rather than dying with these." His head jerked toward the other three women.

If we kept this up, he was going to pat my head. His condescension was overwhelming.

"I know exactly what it is. The facet of death. It wasn't made for you, and you shouldn't have it. As for that other nonsense, you can shove it," I said.

Tomas' eyes widened, and his face creased in anger. He didn't speak, just stepped out of the sandstorm and slapped my hand away from the seal. "This is mine," he snarled.

"No!" I heard either Panya or Nonna scream.

I pushed against Tomas, trying to get the seal before he did.

There was a roar somewhere in the distance, a masculine scream, and then I was blasted away from where I stood. I had no idea whether I had the seal, or what was happening.

When I pushed myself up, I was in the kitchen, closer to the sliding glass door, and the whirling sand was gone.

In its place stood a prowling panther. He stopped moving, and slowly moved his large head, his golden eyes meeting mine.

"Logan," I breathed.

Then I screamed as a cold nose nudged my arm.

A wolf the size of a small car stood next to me.

One of the other women called out something in a language I didn't understand, and both the wolf and the panther froze.

"Wynter, are you all right?" Farrah called out.

"Do you have the seal?" That was from Panya.

I slowly held my hand up closer to my face. In it was the seal. I didn't remember getting hold of it, but I thanked my lucky stars I had.

"Who was that?" Nonna asked me as she came over to help me up.

"Tomas Severn, who has no business being involved in this," I said, my mind reeling. What would the man who was possibly part of harming Evander Thane be doing with a seal—a facet of power, a strong magical object—of an ancient Egyptian sect of madmen?

Whatever he was doing, it wasn't good.

"Thank the goddess," Nonna sagged against the island. "I was afraid he got it."

"Who are the shifters?" Panya asked.

"What are the shifters?" Farrah breathed, her chest heaving. "Jeez, those things are real? Why didn't they eat us?"

"Shifters don't eat people," Nonna said absently. "Do you know them, Wynter?"

"I know the panther," I said. "Maybe you could let them go, or unfreeze them, or whatever. Oh," I got to my feet. "They're going to be naked as can be, so I need to get some sheets, or something," I made a move toward the other side of my now trashed living room, to the hallway where the linen closet was.

"They're naked?" I heard behind me in what sounded like a scandalized whisper.

That made me giggle, although I was way beyond humor. This must be shock, I thought.

I pulled two sheets from the closet and went back into the living room. "Okay, can we let them go?"

Panya waved a hand, and both animals were snarling, looking around.

"He's gone," I said to the panther, hoping it was Logan. If it wasn't, this was going to go from bad to worse. "You can change. I have a sheet for both of you, since I take it the wolf is with you?"

The panther eyed me, his golden eyes staring, unblinking.

"I don't know where your clothes are," I said, wiping my forehead. Apparently, grave danger didn't deter the damn hot flash. I was dying over here. "Take it or leave it. I need some water." I dropped a sheet in front of the panther, and then one in front of the wolf, although I kept a distance. Then I got a glass of water and drank every drop.

Everyone was looking at me, even the panther and the wolf.

"What? Hot flash. You want to talk about it?" I snapped, tired of everything.

There was a whooshing sound, and then the animals were gone, and two men stood in their place, fumbling with the sheet. Logan wrapped his around his waist. But the other man was expertly tying a toga.

"Wynter, thank you. This is Mark Tattersall, my friend. He came back with me. If you recall, I was hoping he would." Logan spoke carefully. "Ladies, we mean you no harm."

"Thanks for the sheet," Mark said. "Logan is right. The only thing we meant to harm was the talking sandstorm. What was that?"

Panya gasped. "It's the facet! The power of will!"

"What?" I asked.

Nonna moved toward her daughter, stopping to stand next to her, both them laser focused on Logan. "It is," Nonna breathed. "The facet of will. How is this possible?" Her question was asked almost of herself versus anyone else.

"What are you talking about?" I asked, moving around the island toward Logan.

Mark beat me there, standing next to Logan.

It was the beginning of a major face off.

My living room wasn't going to survive if the four of them decided to fight.

"What is going on?" Farrah asked.

"As the First Sister, you must join with us," Panya said woodenly. "We must bind the bearer immediately and take the facet before he harms anyone else."

"Whoa! Whoa!" I shouted. "What are you talking about?"

"The panther," Nonna said. "He holds the facet of will. He has the power of the eighth facet."

My mouth opened, but no sound came out.

CHAPTER FOURTEEN

*I*t took me about ten minutes to get everyone to calm down and go to their respective corners. Mark and Logan were still wrapped in sheets, because Nonna and Panya would absolutely not let them leave.

I held the seal.

Farrah stood with her gran and aunt, but she didn't look like she wanted to be blasting anyone.

I got another drink of water. My scalp was sweating. My. Scalp.

This was just not fair.

"Okay," I said. "Let's talk. No magic. No shifting. No attacks. Got it?" I glared at all parties.

There were murmurs of agreement, but they were half-hearted at best.

"What do you mean that Logan has the power of will?" I asked Panya.

She didn't reply to me, but crossed her arms and glared at Logan. "What demon have you been dancing in the crossroads with, panther?"

"What?" Logan gaped at her.

"To be fair, you'd heard that about you in the past," Mark said.

"Not helping," Logan growled.

Mark closed his mouth.

"That is the only way you were able to obtain this facet of power," Panya said. "And only if you got lucky with the demon who was in that crossroads. This is not child's play."

"Lady, I have no idea what you're talking about," Logan said.

This was probably not a good time to admire the line of Logan's shoulders, but I did. And honestly, I felt no regret. Shoulders that lovely deserved to be admired. It was my reward for making it through a pretty vicious hot flash without killing anyone. Normally a patient person, I found that the hot flashes made me varying degrees of homicidal with people's nonsense.

Nonna looked at Panya, and Logan, and then Farrah, and finally me. She seemed to come to some decision. "Will you sit?" she asked Logan. "Then we can explain."

"No more freezing," Mark interjected. "Or hexes of any kind." His voice brooked no discussion.

"I accept your terms," Nonna nodded her head.

"I would like to get my clothes," Logan said. "You can come with me if you like."

"Where are they?" I asked. After Officer Trenton showed up and I made a scene yelling to my neighbors, I didn't need two men in togas roaming the neighborhood.

"They're just out back," Mark said. "We came around the back and shifted. We're used to this," he gave me a smile.

I nodded, accepting their request.

"Panya?" I asked, hoping to get buy in from the Sisters as well.

"I'll walk with them," she said.

The two men and Panya walked out into the backyard. When they came back, both men were in jeans and tee shirts, carrying their shoes.

"Great. This is a good start," I said. "Now can we all sit, and talk without trying to kill each other?"

Mark and Logan sat on the loveseat. They were wary, and on edge. But they were dressed, which hopefully meant that they didn't plan to shift any time soon.

I glanced outside. It was late afternoon. This scrying certainly took a long time. I should be hungry, I thought, but I wasn't.

"Water?" I asked, as an excuse to go and get myself some more water. Without waiting for an answer, I went back to the kitchen, filled the pitcher, and my glass, and brought it all over on one of my trays.

Everyone was silent as they poured themselves some water. This was good. People were less likely to get all drastic in their actions when they were holding food and drink. I'd noticed this early on in my volunteering life. I figured it couldn't hurt to try it in my new magical life.

And if it kept my poor living room from getting trashed further, all the better. The sand was never coming out, I thought as I looked down at the rug.

"Okay, Nonna, this would be a good time to explain about… everything," I waved a hand vaguely to encompass all that had happened in the last couple of days.

So Nonna, with Panya, explained to Logan and Mark who they were, what they were doing, and about the facets of power held by the Fathers of the Desert.

"You think Logan has one of these?" Mark asked, his skepticism clear.

"I know he does," Panya. "We are the Sisters of the Asp. We can sense the facets. It's our purpose now—to sense them and keep them safely locked away."

"Well, you haven't done a great job," Logan said. "If I do, in fact, have this thing."

"We've lost most of the Sisterhood in the past ten years," Nonna said. "Each Sister had a tomb that she guarded. But with each death, the tombs became less guarded. Which was the plan. Humans, even magical humans, couldn't get past all our wards. Demons, however," she sighed, leaning back. "We didn't plan for that."

"Why not?" Farrah asked.

"The Fathers of the Desert, for all their power, were just men. Mere men," Panya said. "But they figured out how to use demons to break through."

"I wonder why a demon had the facet of will, rather than one of the people who was seeking it," I said, thinking of Tomas Severn.

"Demons are very clever, and very opportunistic," Mark said.

"Then why did you go see a demon?" Farrah asked Logan.

"I don't know," he shrugged. "I don't remember anything past seven years ago."

"We need to get Tomas back here," I said. "He wants the seal. Let's use it to lure him here and get some answers from him."

The silence that lay on the room after my words was heavier than water.

"What? Am I completely off base?" I asked.

"And what do we do when we get him here?" Farrah asked.

"We bind him, and ask him questions," I said.

"And what? Torture him?" Mark asked, one corner of his mouth tilting up.

I got the impression the idea didn't bother him all that much.

"No!" I said. "But he's the one who is going to be desperate, right? If we took his toy," I waved my hand still holding the seal. "Then he wants it back."

"We're going to need to call him," Farrah said slowly. "If we're the ones who keep track of the facets. We'll be able to find him, right?" She looked at her gran and her aunt.

"We should be able to," Nonna said.

"May I make a suggestion?" I asked.

Everyone turned to me.

"Why don't we let him stew a little? I need a shower. I have to clean this room. It's making me crazy. I'm starving. Let's eat, and if you all will help me clean up, I'll get us the best Chinese on the island. We may not need to call him. He may come to us. Could you sense that?" I asked the Sisters.

"Even though he doesn't have the seal, he has the connection to the facet of death," Nonna said.

"What do we do if he shows up?" Farrah asked.

"You're going to need to bind him," Panya said to her niece.

"I don't know how," Farrah said.

"We can show you. You're strong, and I think you'll manage it," Nonna said.

"Wynter, I think this is a great idea," Logan smiled at me.

I felt myself blush under the warmth of his smile. I didn't realize how much I'd missed him. And while seeing him in a sheet was delightful, I hadn't had a chance to process how happy his return made me. Not until now, when I was sure my guests wouldn't be trying to kill each other. Or burn down my house.

"Okay, will you help me clean? You can all stay here tonight," I said, getting up. "So that you can all be sure no one else is involved in any funny business."

With that, a sort of cease fire settled across everyone in my home. Nonna was aggressive with the vacuum. I thought there might be a chance that I could be sand free after a year or so.

After an hour, we were done. I called my favorite Chinese restaurant and essentially ordered one of everything (the shifters were looking a little long in the tooth. I figured I'd better).

When the food arrived, we all sat down at the table.

"Logan, why don't you remember most of your life?" Farrah asked as she ate.

Logan told the story of being found in the Mohave Desert, covered in cuts and wounds, and close to death. Mark interjected to add to the story.

"Mark's the one who recognized that I was good at finding things," Logan said.

"In a way that seems impossible?" Panya asked.

"Sometimes," he said reluctantly.

"That is the facet of will. You bend the world to your will," Panya said. "You have sold your soul for something you cannot keep."

"What do you mean?" I asked.

"Crossroads demons take nothing less than a soul," Farrah was the one who answered. "There is very little else they'll accept. I've heard of a few exceptions but only when the seeker had something very unique that the demon wanted."

"How do you know this?" I asked.

"Magical law enforcement?" Farrah asked. "Hello?"

I nodded. I wondered what it would take for Farrah's quest to be fulfilled. I had no idea. I thought I'd feel something when I saw her mom, when I did what her mom asked, but I hadn't felt a thing. In fact, I felt compelled to still help Farrah.

So obviously I wasn't done.

But what would it take? This was larger than anything I'd expected. Than anyone expected. A cursed group of women who'd been systematically murdered. Two groups of people who used to be allies, and who were now bitter enemies.

Plus all the anger and mistrust sitting around my dinner table.

Logan was stunned at the revelation he'd apparently sold his soul as Evander. I remembered talking to him about Evander, and he'd said that there were rumors of shady deals and behavior. This was a lot more than shady.

"If you were secret, and the Fathers of the Desert were all dead, how did the demons or anyone else find out about you?" I asked, following a train of thought.

Everyone looked at me. Oops. I must have tossed this out in the middle of a different discussion.

"That's a good question," Mark said. "How did a couple of secret societies become something that people know about?"

"I don't know," Nonna said. "If I did, it would make things easier. We could trace how we were exposed."

"Would someone in the Sisters of the Asp have told?" Farrah asked.

"I want to say no, but I am not sure of anything anymore," Nonna said. "I never thought I'd see the day when there were only three of us." She rested her chin on her folded hands.

"That's something to ask Tomas," I said. "How did they find out? And Logan?"

He turned toward me.

"I know you don't want to believe the demon thing but remember my visions? There were two women and men always around you. Even Tomas, who was obviously not part of your close circle, was laser focused on you. Everyone there was. Maybe the rumors were more widely known than you realized."

He was nodding. "That's a good point, as much as I don't want to admit it. Someone knew what I'd gotten from the demon."

"The fact that Tomas had the facet of death adds to that."

"Where's the facet Logan is supposed to have?" Mark asked. "If the seal, or whatever that thing is," he jerked his chin at me, since I still held the seal, "Is what gives the power, where's Logan's power? I can tell you, he didn't have a seal on him when I found him."

"Another good question. I'd bet you hid it," I looked at Logan. "That sounds true to character."

"But you need contact with the seal. To have the power, you must have the physical thing that embodies the facet," Nonna said.

"I was reputed to be pretty clever," Logan said, leaning back as he rubbed his thumb and forefinger along his jaw. "Maybe I found a loophole."

"You're good at it," Mark said.

"You can't keep it," Nonna said. "There can be no facets of power in the world. Even one is too much."

"But—" Logan started to protest.

"She's right," Farrah said. "Even one allows for something to be out in the world, tempting people. We can't risk it."

Logan wouldn't meet anyone's eyes. He got up, carrying his plate to the sink. Then he walked out into the backyard, the door gaping open into the darkness of his wake.

"There's no other way?" Mark asked, meeting the gaze of each of the Sisters one at a time.

"No," Nonna said.

Panya shook her head.

I got up and went out back.

Logan was standing toward the back of my yard, his hands on his hips, legs spread, his entire body radiating anger.

"Hey," I said.

"I am finally finding myself," he said, his voice low and raspy. "For seven years, I've operated in the dark, unaware of who I was, or why I was left to die. Just as truth begins to come to light, I'm finding out my truth is not only bad, it's complete crap. And someone wants to take part of it away from me."

"I don't know that you want this part," I said.

"I don't know that I do or don't," he turned to look at me. His eyes blazed golden, a sure sign of his inner turmoil. "I want to make that decision on my own."

"The man you used to be was not the best of men," I began. I needed to choose my words with care. "You know this. The rumors alone have shown you this. If you don't want to be that man again, then you need to make changes so that you're not that man."

"What does that leave me?" Logan asked.

"I don't know. I like the man Logan Gentry is," I said. "I always have. I'm less sure about Evander Thane." I stood next to him, my arms crossed in front of me.

So quickly that I didn't have time to react, Logan turned and folded me into his arms, his embrace nearly overwhelming me. He smelled so good, he felt good… my senses swam.

Then his hands came up to cup my face, and his lips were on mine. Full and firm and warm. He leaned into me.

My knees wobbled.

As quickly as I'd been encompassed by Logan, he let me go.

"But I have no soul," he whispered.

Then he leapt over the fence and was gone.

I stared.

Oh, no.

When I was able to move again, I walked back to the house, but Panya and Nonna were already at the door.

"Where is he?" Panya demanded. She took one look at my face and whirled around. "You gave your word, and now he's gone!" she shouted at Mark.

"I'll find him," Mark said.

"You're not going anywhere," Farrah said.

"I'm your best bet to not only find him but bring him back," Mark was unperturbed by the anger flying at him. "I'll give you my word as a wolf that I will come back, and I will bring Logan with me."

"Your word," Panya scoffed.

Mark glared at her. The wolf glared out from behind his eyes.

"I accept," Nonna said, stepping in front of her daughter, putting out her hand. "Your word. Your solemn bond."

Mark nodded, and bit his hand. Blood bloomed in his palm.

I covered my mouth to stifle my gasp.

Nonna whipped a small knife out from her pocket and slashed her own palm.

The two of them clasped palms and then held them close with the other hand.

"So it is sworn," they said together.

What happened to the idea that you didn't give up your blood? This was serious doings.

"I'll bring him back," Mark said. He smiled at me.

Did he know what had just happened? I was still stunned, not only because Logan had bailed, but because of his touching me. His kiss. My entire body was still tingling, still jumping with the electricity of his touch.

Mark walked out in the backyard, closing the door behind him.

"Well, that went well," Panya said.

"It's a hiccup," I said. "We still need to see if we can get a hold of Tomas. I still can't believe that vapid man I danced with is holding one of these power thingys."

Have Farrah call for him, Goldie spoke for the first time in hours.

What?

Farrah is the First Sister. As such, she has a special connection to the Fathers of the Desert. Even if the facets are not held by the original Fathers, their essence is present. Have Farrah call them.

Okay, I thought. Then I relayed Goldie's words to the other women.

Nonna was nodding even before I finished. "The First Sister has always had an extra connection to the Fathers. She was initially their conduit to the Sisters. The bridge, if you will. It could work," she looked at Farrah. "You can do this."

"I trust you," Farrah said.

"Then let's do it. The sooner we get this Tomas person, the better," Panya said, her tone impatient and her movements those of one who is deeply angry.

We all sat in my living room. I hoped that Tomas wouldn't show up with a sandstorm again.

Farrah, Nonna, and Panya sat together, hands clasped. Seeing them close together, and so still showed me how similar they all looked. All three regal and beautiful.

I didn't know how long they sat together, not speaking. I dozed, and I jerked myself awake. They were still sitting together, legs crossed, in the middle of the living room. I hadn't moved the coffee table back after the witches left, so they had plenty of room.

What I wanted to do was go get a shower—that had yet to happen—and lie in bed and think about Logan, but he had to wait.

When I looked around, I could practically see the magic in the air. There was also a strong scent of herbs. Interesting. I didn't know that magic could take on a feel and a smell.

"You're doing great, Wynter," Florry said.

I whipped around, but I couldn't see her. "Where are you?" I whispered.

"I'm not showing up. Those dames will sense me quick as can be. I don't want to expose me or you. But I'm watching over you, and you're doing great. Keep it up. And keep drinking water. I'd hate to see you off one of them because you were sweaty."

I rolled my eyes, but didn't say anything. Hopefully, none of the Sisters noticed.

Florry didn't speak again, so I assumed she'd left. But it was nice that she was watching. She was paying attention, and if things were going to go sideways for me, maybe she'd be there to warn me.

The house jumped.

"What the heck?" I whisper shrieked, leaping from the chair.

The women on the floor were on their feet.

"I think you got his attention," I said.

"Indeed," a man walked into the kitchen through my hallway. It was Tomas Severn. "I heard the call of the First Sister. What does the defeated leader of a decimated order want with one of the Fathers of the Desert?" His tone was proud, dismissive.

But he was here.

Which meant he needed to be here. Otherwise someone like this would have ignored Farrah.

Into a chair, I thought, staring hard at him. *Into. A. Chair.*

I felt a headache forming behind my eyes.

Nothing happened.

Damn it.

Get in the chair! I'm hot, tired, I want a shower, and I don't have time for your nonsense! I thought.

Tomas Severn flew sideways, landing in one of the dining room chairs so hard that he knocked it over.

"Now!" I shouted.

Panya and Nonna sprang into action, sparks of green light coming from their fingertips. Tomas Severn was bound in green glowing bonds before he could start yelling.

But he did start to yell, and whatever it was, it made Nonna pale. "We must silence him," she said to Farrah and Panya, not paying attention to me.

They clasped hands, and Nonna chanted something I couldn't understand.

Tomas' mouth clamped shut. His face went red, and his eyes bugged out of his head.

I knew I should feel bad, but what I was thinking was, Was that what I looked like in the midst of a hot flash? Please, sweet baby Jee, no.

"You will not speak. You will not move. You will do nothing that unless we permit it," Nonna said, her voice hard. "You have brought forth that which desecrated the earth before. You have no care for others, for this world, for nothing other than your own gain. That ends now."

Tomas' face went pale, and he narrowed his eyes at Nonna.

"We need to bind him," Nonna said.

"My pleasure," Panya said, grinning. "Help me sit him up." Together, Farrah and Panya got the chair upright. "Your bad deeds are done," she said to Tomas.

Waving a hand over her open palm, a reddish gold glow formed. I could see that it was an Arabic letter. I wondered what it did.

Tomas knew, apparently, because his eyes went wide and he struggled against his glowing bonds. It was to no avail. Panya dropped the glowing character over top of him. His struggles ceased, and his head dropped forward.

"It takes a couple of minutes for the spell to work," Nonna said. "Then he will be unable to cast any spells against us."

"Um, you are more than a little scary," I whispered.

"Good," she whispered back. "These sorts need to be scared."

It felt like forever before Tomas raised his head.

"Are you ready to talk?" Panya asked.

Slowly, Tomas nodded.

onna released the gag spell she'd cast on Tomas.

"It's no use," Tomas spat immediately. "I will never betray my order."

"Whatever," Farrah said. "Your kind always say that, and a life of living is always better than being dead in the ground."

Whoa. Where had that come from?

"What are you offering?" Tomas asked, a predatory gleam in his eye.

"You tell us what we want to know, and you get to live," Farrah leaned closer to him. "Sound fair?"

"Death is not the end," Tomas said. "Try again." His lips twisted in a sneer.

"We need to compel him," Panya said. "He will only lie otherwise."

"Wait, what? What does that mean?" I asked. "To compel?"

"It's the magical equivalent of a truth serum," Tomas said. "You seem like a decent woman. What kind of practitioner compels another?" He shook his head dramatically.

"Shut up," I said. Such blatant rudeness would make my mother turn in her grave, but I was done.

"There's no other way," Panya said. She nodded at her mom.

The two women turned to face Tomas, and both spoke softly.

I felt the weave of magic in the air. I wanted to protest, but I hated to admit that they were right. What did that make me? How did you keep your personal ethics when dealing with this kind of person?

"That's better," Panya said, satisfaction dripping from the two words. "Now, let's talk, Mr. Severn."

"Sure, but it won't help you," Tomas said with a leer.

"How did you find out about the facets?" Nonna asked.

Whatever he'd been expecting, that hadn't been it. Tomas' eyebrows rose toward his hairline. "How? The scroll."

"Goddess," Panya said.

"What?" I asked.

"Part of the scrolls of our history were stolen. Not many, but enough, apparently," Nonna said as she glared at Tomas.

"After that, it was easy. We only had to trace the magical residue into the deep desert," Tomas said, sounding proud. "It took more time to break through the charms, but with some help," he grinned unpleasantly, "We broke them. And when we found each tomb of the Fathers, our knowledge grew. We're almost complete," he boasted.

"Why were you after Logan at his party before he disappeared?" I asked.

"Because he has one of the facets," Tomas said simply.

"Why did you leave him in the desert to die?"

"He wasn't supposed to die. One of our... questioners got overly enthusiastic in his tasks, and he bit Evander.

He was—is—a shifter, and we were worried what someone like Evander would do if he woke up and shifted. So we left him in the desert to go through the change."

"You nearly killed him."

"Trust me, we paid for our mistake. We had the power of will right there, in our hands—" Tomas shook his head.

"Why didn't you just take it?" I asked.

He looked at me. "You cannot take a facet. It must be freely given, gifted if you will. If he dies, the power returns to the demon he got it from. Or maybe the Father the demon took it from. We're not sure. We needed Evander alive, so he could gift the facet to one more deserving. One with proper vision," he sneered.

I turned away then. I didn't want to hear anymore. The Sisters of the Asp could handle this. I'd need to tell Logan what I'd learned—that he was accidentally turned. That he was left there to shift so they could wring what they wanted out of him.

Somehow, it felt worse than knowing he'd been left there to die.

"Where is he now?" Tomas called. "We are getting close. We need to find him!"

"You will never find him," I said in a voice I didn't recognize as my own. I walked into the kitchen, unable to get a hold on the anger Tomas brought out in me.

The sliding glass door opened. Mark came in, followed by Logan.

"As I promised," Mark said.

"That was fast," I said.

"Evander! You're alive!" Tomas shouted from out in the living room. "Thank the gods! We thought you'd been eaten by wild animals!" He laughed then, an evil sounding cackle.

"Don't kill him," I said quickly in Logan's direction. "He's being very helpful, by way of a compelling spell. And I have more to tell you, but let's get through this, okay?" I put my hand on his arm, the touch of him under my hand setting my entire being aflame.

Logan looked at my hand, and then into my eyes.

Oh, good night, Maggie. I was going to drown in those golden green eyes. "I trust you," he said. Then he looked toward Tomas, and the Sisters. "But I can't be around them. Any of them."

"You don't need to," I said. "Your room is yours. Go. I'll come and see you later."

Logan strode off without another word.

"I'll stay with him," Mark said. "It's going to be fine, Wynter." Then Mark, too, disappeared upstairs.

"Hey! No! Where are you going? You can't leave!" Tomas wailed.

I walked back to where the Sisters stood. I didn't want to be here, but I would do this for Logan.

They questioned Tomas for another hour, but he didn't have much more to give. Why anyone would give absolute power to a carrot head like this was beyond me, but I wasn't an evil villain intent on taking over the world, so what did I know?

Panya gagged him again.

"Thank you," I said. "I'm tired of hearing him."

"He does talk too much," she agreed.

"What do we do with him now?" Farrah asked.

"This is where you come in, my little flower, First Sister," Nonna said.

"You need to strip him of the seal and take back the facet. We have the seal, so you pull the power from him."

I took the seal from my pocket and handed it to Farrah.

Tomas' eyes went wide at the sight of the seal, and he bucked in the chair, desperate to get free, to get to the seal. His eyes followed it like a lover. An obsessed lover, one with a couple of restraining orders.

"Do you remember your Arabic?" Nonna asked Farrah.

Farrah nodded.

"Take the seal in your hands. Hold your hands over it, encompassing it."

Farrah clasped the seal between her hands.

"Now focus on the facet, on the power of death, a power this man has taken, and repeat after me," Nonna said. "Arjie aly khudh mink."

"What does it mean?" I whispered to Panya.

"Return to me, take from thee," she whispered out of the side of her mouth. "Simple and easy and direct."

"Oh," I said. "I thought it had to be given freely."

"To use it, yes. If Farrah wanted to be able to use the power of the facet, Tomas would need to give it to her. But to merely take it and seal it away? That can be removed from him. Which is better, actually. We don't want anyone to be able to use it."

"So that fixes it?" I asked, my mood lightening a little.

"Perhaps. The facets were never supposed to be able to be found, much less removed from the tombs of the Fathers of the Desert. It seems like a mistake to rule anything out."

"Makes sense," I agreed glumly. That was definitely a downer.

Nonna and Farrah were chanting the Arabic phrase over and over, and Tomas was straining within his bonds. It was clear he didn't want to give up the power of death.

Too damn bad.

Tomas screamed behind the gag spell, and a white light shot out toward Farrah. It landed on her hands, and she tumbled backward.

Tomas went limp in the chair. Nonna kneeled down to help Farrah, who sat up, her hands still gripping the seal.

"I got it," she said. Her hair had come out of her tie, and it was curling all around her face. Farrah looked tired, but she was beaming. "I felt it," she said. "I felt it jump out of him, and into the seal. So now what?"

"We must return with the seal to Egypt, and bury it once more, away from not only the eyes and reach of men, but that of demons as well," Panya said. Her gaze fell upon me. "We will be returning with two seals."

"Oh, lord," I said. "I don't know—"

"It is not his," Panya said, and her voice was gentler than it had been since the first time I met her. "He cannot keep it."

"I know," I whispered. I was so sad for Logan. They hadn't seen his face when he talked about losing a past he'd only just found. Good or bad, it was his. And now, part of it would be taken from him.

Although personally, I thought that getting rid of the murderous Fathers' facets wasn't a bad thing. But I figured Logan didn't want to hear such rational ideas at the moment. "I can go and get him."

"There is no need," Nonna said. "We need to send this one somewhere. Somewhere that he can do no harm, and where his compatriots will not easily find him. Then we should all sleep, and we can talk with Logan tomorrow."

"Where do you suggest we send Tomas?" I asked. "I mean, somewhere that he can do as little harm as possible."

"Why don't we send him to Uncle Tarak?" Panya asked. "Uncle can keep an eye on him and keep him from further mischief. We just need to get him there."

"Give me a description of your uncle, his home, where you want him to go," I said.

"I'll show you," Nonna said. She came to me and took my hand in hers. "Come with me," she said.

When her fingers curled around mine, I was pulled into a place I'd never seen before. A sunny afternoon in a market town. It was not desert, but nor was it a plush oasis. It was something in between. Cars and donkeys fought for space on the narrow road. Women called for their children, with sellers of fruits, vegetables, animals in cages, sunglasses, purses, and hats all crammed together. And off to one side, I felt Nonna's focus. A tall man, thin, with a neatly trimmed beard, and sitting at a folding table under a canopy with a laptop. He was talking with a man who was gesturing wildly with his hands, nodding at the man's words.

"Uncle Tarak," Nonna said. "Send him there. Panya, give him a call so he knows what to expect."

"Okay, I think I have it," I said. "I'm not perfect at this, and he's bigger than a pot." I stared at Tomas. Please, please, please let this work.

I closed my eyes, seeing the market space, hearing the sounds, smelling the dust, and cooking food, and the animals and the heat. "Go," I said. "Go there now."

When I opened my eyes, Tomas Severn was gone. I hoped he landed safely.

"Well done," Nonna said. "Why don't you get some sleep, and we'll come back to you tomorrow?"

I nodded. Hugging all three of them, I saw them out. Then I wearily climbed the stairs and fell into bed with my clothes on. This had to be the longest day of my life, and that included when I met my husband's other wife.

Tomorrow promised to be a doozy as well.

How in the heck was I going to share all this with Logan? More specifically, how to get him to agree?

I texted Shelly to let her know I was alive and in one piece, but when she asked if I wanted to talk, I declined. There was too much within me that couldn't settle, and I didn't want to try to talk through it. It took a long time for me to fall asleep that night.

CHAPTER SIXTEEN

*I*t was a full day before the three Sisters returned to my house. Farrah texted and told me there was work to be done to protect the facet before traveling.

Logan and Mark stayed upstairs most of the day. Logan came down for coffee and food around noon—I knew that he'd have to come out to eat eventually—and I shared with him what we'd learned about him from Tomas. His face went as dark as a thundercloud, and my heart broke for him.

He stormed upstairs without another word.

"He'll be all right. He's not one who is used to the word 'no'," Mark said. "The later you have to learn it, the more it stings." He smiled and went upstairs.

That was a very astute observation. Evander certainly didn't take no for an answer, and Logan avoided the word no with some regularity. Was that the power of will, the power of the facet, or was that Evander-Logan himself?

I guess we'd find out.

I took the time to call Caro, and relay the message from Florry. That she was to get her poop in a pile and come to see me. Stay for a while. The fact that I was able to speak those words without dissolving into laughter so intense I cried, and maybe peed my pants was the closest thing to a miracle I'd ever seen.

When the ladies came back, Farrah was the first one in the door. She looked tired, but happy.

"Hey," I said. "How goes it?"

"It goes well. There's a lot going," Farrah replied.

"That's good to hear," I said, happy for her. "Care to share?"

"I'm leaving magical law enforcement," she said. "I can't work with Panya and Nonna and keep a day job. When they go back to Egypt, I'm going with them. I called my boss and quit."

"What did they say?"

"Remember those creative name callings I told you about you?" Farrah asked.

I smiled. "What will you tell your dad?"

"I already told him. I told him I wanted to get to know Mom's family, and he said he thought that would be great. He was happy for me." She beamed with pleasure.

"What about the seals? The facets?" I said.

"Once we collect the facet of will, we will have two of the facets. That means that those who seek them are actually seeking three. The facet of time is still safely hidden. We will return the facets to their resting place, and place strong safeguards on them," Nonna said, coming from behind Farrah and resting an arm on Farrah's waist.

Farrah leaned her head down toward the hijab of her grandmother.

"Then we will hunt down those who have stolen the other five and return them as well. With three of us, with a First Sister—"

Panya glanced at her mother and her niece. Something in her face was off, and it worried me. But what could it be?

"—we will be able to do the work that is our calling."

"Yes, we will," Farrah agreed.

Panya looked even more worried.

"I'm sorry, but we need Logan," Nonna said.

"Let me go get him," I said.

I ran up the stairs to the spare room. How both Logan and Mark had fit in there last night was a mystery, but I'd let it be. I'd been too tired to manage anything more than falling into bed, which I'd done spectacularly, if I do say so myself. I knocked on the door.

"Logan?" I called.

The door swung open. "Are they here?" he asked.

I nodded.

"Then let's do it." He strode off down the hall, and then I heard him on the stairs.

"He's fine," Mark said.

"I'm glad you think so," I said.

"You're good to worry for him. But he's a good man, no matter who he was before, and he'll do the right thing. He always has," Mark said simply.

"Even in business?" I asked, starting down the stairs.

"Oh, well, business is a different matter," Mark said, laughing softly.

"Hmm," I said.

Logan was standing in front of the three Sisters. "What do you want me to do?" he asked.

"You must offer up the facet of power, and gift the power of will to Farrah," Nonna said.

He nodded once, sharp and all business. "Let's do this." He seemed to have a limited vocabulary today.

Farrah took Logan's hands. I wondered why she didn't clasp her hands together, and I remembered that she didn't have the seal for Logan's facet. Would it just fall out of the sky? Maybe my flying pots weren't all that abnormal.

"I gift to you the power of will, the facet of power given to me," Logan said. He repeated it four more times, and then a white light flashed between them.

Unlike before, Farrah was prepared for the impact, and she didn't fall backward, but instead, braced herself. When she opened her hand, she had a small gold and blue seal with the design of a lion on it.

Logan slumped a little. "It's done?"

"It is done." Nonna came to him and put her hands on his shoulders. "I know this was hard for you. But you have done the right thing, and your sacrifice will help restore order. If it makes you feel any better, those who harmed you will not find success. Not now, when you have given us the facet of will. They will lose, Logan, and it is directly because of your actions."

He looked up then. "That eases the sting a little. But I'm still bound to a demon."

"I cannot help you with that. Should I come across something that might help, I will work to help you. That's all I can offer you," Nonna said.

"Thank you," he said.

Behind them, Panya let out a whoop.

"What?" I looked to see what it was.

She was looking at Farrah, who had her hands on a new necklace. Made of gold, and turquoise, it lay around her neck. In the middle was a small, turquoise scarab.

"She's got the choker!" Panya said.

"What does this mean?" I asked the room at large.

"It means that the First Sister has passed on the mantle of her place. While Anipe gave Farrah her power, she didn't fully hand over the responsibility of the First Sister. The necklace means that Anipe has passed it to Farrah and moved to the beyond."

"I won't see her again?" Farrah looked startled.

"You never should have seen her after she passed. You were fortunate to be able to do so. It's not the natural order of things," Nonna said. "We were concerned that something was truly awry, because the necklace should have come when your mother gave you her gifts. But she was protecting us to the end," she kissed her lips and looked up at the ceiling.

"You mean she didn't trust me," Farrah said, her brows furrowing.

"No, she was protecting both you and the Sisters," Panya said. "Something your mother was especially good at."

With that, I felt something click into place. "You don't need me anymore," I said.

"What?" Farrah turned to me.

"I have fulfilled your quest. You know what happened to your mother, and you have been able to put it to rest."

"How can you know?" Farrah asked.

"I know," I said, thinking of Florry's words. She was right. I'd know. And I did.

Within the hour, Farrah, Nonna, and Panya were saying their goodbyes. They'd heard from Uncle Tarak, who was keeping Tomas busy. It was not a forever solution, but it was one that would keep him from the people he worked with for a time. There was nothing left to do but to say goodbye.

Had Nonna not brought it up, I would have forgotten the idea of payment entirely. This had been the wildest week of my life. I felt at least one hundred years older, and I was sweating like someone one hundred; payment was the last thing on my mind.

She gave me a bracelet with a scarab on it, and told me to wear it on my left wrist, to protect me along my heart line. She didn't look at Logan when she said it, but I felt the warning.

Which I didn't want to hear. I'd dreamed of his kiss last night.

Then Panya produced a larger burner basin of polished brass. It was beautiful, and would allow for me to spread the herbal mixtures out more.

Finally, Nonna gave me an envelope, and told me to open it later. A last round of hugs and kisses, even for Logan and Mark, and they were gone.

"And you're just letting them leave, with all they still have to do?" Logan asked, his expression dark.

"Their journey isn't mine," I said.

"How can you know? This is huge, this whole thing."

"Yes, but this is their calling. Mine is to help people as they come to me. Not take on the quest of another," I said.

Mark excused himself.

"Wynter, about the other night—" Logan began.

"It's fine," I said. "No worries. No hard feelings."

"No, that's not it at all," he said, frowning.

I moved away from him into the kitchen, not wanting to hear anymore. I started to do the dishes when I felt him come up behind me. His arms slipped around my waist.

"What I am trying to tell you is that I'd like to do it again," he said. "If you'll stand still long enough, woman."

"Oh," I said. "Oh." I stopped, with my hands still in the sink.

"Wynter?"

I turned and wrapped my arms around his neck, pulling him toward me, finding his embrace even better now, now that he was not wrapped in sorrow and anger.

He kissed me again, gently, tenderly, and then with increasing hunger. It was glorious to be wanted, to be desired—and by someone that I desired just as much.

Neither of us heard the door, or the footsteps in the hall. I could barely remember my own name.

But my blood ran cold when I heard the outraged tones of my daughter.

"Mom! What in the name of crazy is going on here?"

The End

I hope you enjoyed the latest story with Wynter, as well as the whatever-it-is that is happening with Logan. I didn't mean to leave it like this, but I could see it so

clearly in my head that after reading it a couple of times, I decided this was where I wanted to end it. The story picks up in Necromancy & Nightsweats. As always, you can find my work on Amazon.

Four weeks ago, a dead man washed ashore. Four days ago, his body disappeared from the morgue. Four hours ago, I was accused of his murder. Unfortunately for me, my last nerve drowned in the sea of my new friend named night sweats.

Just when I thought it was safe to step onto my porch, the power of the Oracle has sent another person in need to my stairs. He thinks he's searching for his missing husband, but the moment I smell him, I know he's dragging along a curse from a necromancer with a stench strong enough to curl the leg hairs I haven't had time to shave.

Which reminds me—I should probably do some lady grooming before my date.

And did I mention I have an arraignment in court? For murder? It's all I can do to put this legal nonsense to bed before the rotten bouquet of necromancy wafts into my world yet again.

If one more person says that age is just an number, they're going to wish they'd disappeared with my last nerve.

One Click Necromancy & Night Sweats

Want to keep up with the latest releases from Lisa Manifold? Sign up for my Newsletter... www.lisamanifold.com/news

Love the strong older women with more than a little magic? Then you'll love The Deadwood Sisters. They may look like twenty-somethings, but in reality, they are more like one-hundred and twenty. They protect Deadwood. No exceptions.

Are you a mystery fan who likes your suspense with a touch of romance? Then check out The Mostly Open Paranormal Investigative Agency series, complete with a witch, a vampire, and a maddening demon and where being cursed is a family affair.

Don't miss a release, a sneak peak, cover reveals, and more. Sign up for my Newsletter!

Thank you so much for being a reader, and spreading the word, which includes telling a friend. Reviews are how readers find new books and new authors to love. Please leave a review on your favorite book site.

XO,

Lisa

Turn the page for an excerpt from the first book in the Deadwood Sisters series, Hellborn.

Chapter One

The sound of breaking china echoed around the house as I slammed out the front door. I made sure to slam the screen door hard, just to make a point.

"Damn woman," I muttered.

"I heard that!"

"Good!" I yelled over my shoulder. "I wanted you to!" I stomped to my car, pulling my keys from my pocket. As I got into the car, I pulled my hair up into a messy bun. I caught sight of myself in the mirror. Dark brown hair, brownish green eyes, and the nose ring. I couldn't get used to it, but I needed it to look like someone else. The only thing that would cure me now was to race down the road in my Porsche 911. Speed was a universal healer.

Or killer, if you weren't careful. But it didn't matter. I couldn't die. More's the damn pity. The nose ring sparkled in the sunlight. Having to look like someone else was one of the joys of not being able to die. "I hate my life."

"I heard that!" came from the house again.

As I gunned the engine, I saw our neighbor, Mrs. Kittrick, glaring. She hated us. And for this, she'd probably call the cops. Noise complaints were her favorite bitch move. Like we didn't have Sturgis here every damn year. But gotta call the po-po on those Nightingale ... women.

That's how she referred to us. Those Nightingale... women. You could feel the pause. I knew that she wanted to call us whores. But she couldn't bring herself to do it. As the supposed daughter of myself, I was another one in a long line of those ... women.

Which made me nice as pie to her. It nearly killed the old bat.

"Hi, Mrs. Kittrick!" I called out the window as I pulled away from the house. "Your yard is gorgeous, as usual!" I waved like we weren't bitter foes and grinned as I looked in the rear-view mirror to see her glaring at my amazing gunmetal gray automotive ass.

That simple act of petty kindness alone eased my anger and brought it down to a non-killing level.

My sisters were enough to make anyone homicidal. Add my mom to the mix, and it was a miracle that our house was still standing. Four women who were never, ever wrong was challenging on a good day. The small fact that we'd been here for over one hundred and twenty years didn't help, either.

That whole 'can't die' thing was a pain in my ass. But if we left the area, we lost the immortal factor that had allowed us to live here and threaten one another for over a century. We'd only had one of my sisters leave the Deadwood area, and she'd died over sixty years ago. The rest of us stayed here, fussing and fighting, as my mom said.

As I left the neighborhood, and got out onto the highway, I hit the gas, letting the RPMs vent all my frustration. Normally, my family and I resolved our disagreements easily, but not this time. This one was too big.

You can't just ignore it when a necromancer moves into your street. You just can't. They have their craft, like everyone else. But their craft involves the dead. That's where they get their power from—the dead. Hence the 'necro' part of necromancer.

Not to mention I'd never met a single necromancer who did his thing for the good of humanity. Nope. They were always self-centered. Usually raging narcissists, and they exploited the dead. Generally, the dead want to be left in peace, but necromancers are based in holding up that process.

So ... no. No ignoring the friendly neighborhood necromancer. Not on my watch.

My mom—known as Meema--didn't agree. She'd been the one throwing the china at me as I left. My sisters, Deirdre and Daniella, didn't feel strongly one way or the other, but they were tired. So they took the path of least resistance.

Which wasn't the path I was advocating. It had escalated from there. Meema wanted to wait and see if he managed to make things troublesome.

I hated to wait and see. This meant that any pets in the neighborhood would disappear suddenly, at the very least. The dead liked to eat when brought back by necromancers. Cats were a favorite. So were nosy dogs.

Not that we had any. But our neighbors did. I didn't even want Mrs. Kittrick's two evil old cats to get eaten. We had a house chicken, but I'd back Evil against a zombie any day of the week.

Three against one meant we were going to wait and see. I didn't understand why we couldn't just go introduce ourselves, and let him know the rules, mainly: One Strike And You're Out.

I shook my head as I blasted down the highway, Bowie wailing from the speakers. This was just making more work for us. We'd have to start a regular patrol of the cemeteries immediately. That was a shit ton of extra work. Keeping the supernatural side of Deadwood, South Dakota on the rails was enough.

Get your copy now!

ACKNOWLEDGMENTS

Once again, here we are! How I love this genre of book, and I really, really really love Wynter. She and Logan surprised me in this one, honestly. This wasn't on my outline, but then in the back yard, it happened, and I was like... OOOOH! There was no way I could leave it out after it (if you know, you know) made an appearance. More of that to come.

I hope you're enjoying Wynter as much as I am. I love writing her coming into her own, figuring out who she is after a lifetime of what she thought was her identity. After the third book, Necromancy & Night Sweats, also available on Amazon, there will be a box set coming out right before Halloween called Girdles & Ghouls. My story is a short story about Wynter called Samhain

& Stretch Marks. You can preorder it HERE. Or find it by the title on Amazon.

Thanks so much for coming along on this ride with me. You all are the best.

XO,

Lisa

ABOUT THE AUTHOR

Lisa Manifold is a *USA Today* Bestselling Author of
fantasy, paranormal, and romance stories. She moved
to Rocky Mountains of Colorado as an adult and has

no plans of living anywhere else. She is a consummate reader, often running late because "Just one more page!"

Lisa is the author of many flavors of paranormal series. She writes what she does in the hopes that one day, the Goblin King will come and take her away. (She's staying, by the way.)

She lives in the mountains of Colorado with her children, and rescued #reddogs and one murder cat.

Stay in touch:
Sign up for her Newsletter and never miss a thing!
Website: www.lisamanifold.com
Or one of the links below.
And hey - if you've read Maximum Security Magic, you can download the free prequel, Undercover Vamp.
Xoxo
Lisa

ALSO BY LISA MANIFOLD

The Oracle of Winter

Hexes & Hot Flashes

Magic & Menopause

Necromancy & Night Sweats (July 2021)

Academy of Supernatural Felons

with Corinne O'Flynn

Maximum Security Magic

Maximum Security Curse

Maximum Security Charm (Summer 2021)

The Mostly Open Paranormal Investigative Agency

Dark Pact

Dark Night

Dark Fates

Deadwood Sisters

Hellborn: The Unlucky Book 1

Hellfire: The Unlucky Book 2

Hellfury: The Unlucky Book 3

The Midnight Coven Stories

(books written with a collective of authors)

A Midnight Coven Anthology

Tempted by Fae

Cursed Coven Series

Wicked Love

Vampire Mates Series

Immortal Darkness

Vampire Brides Series

Forever Blood

The Dragon Thief

Dragon Lost

Dragon Found

The Realm Series

Heart of the Goblin King

To Wed the Goblin King

Realms of the Goblin King

Rise of the Dragon King

The Companion Tales, Volume I

The Companion Tales, Volume II

The Aumahnee Prophecy

with Corinne O'Flynn

Eamonn's Tale

Marigold's Tale

Watchers of the Veil

Defenders of the Realm

Tales From The Veil

with Corinne O'Flynn

The Portal Keepers

The Gimcrackers

Djinn Everlasting

Three Wishes

Forgotten Wishes

Hidden Wishes

Sisters of the Curse

Thea's Tale

One Night at the Ball

Casimir's Journey

Made in the USA
Monee, IL
05 September 2021